'Why am I here?' Sarah breathed.

From behind her Alex said, 'You know why. Because I want you.'

Sarah whispered raggedly, 'I can't go with you, without knowing what . . . what you intend . . . for . . . for us.'

Alex's voice was harsh, low, and his fingers bit into her elbow. 'I imagine it will be a disaster, but we're going to be lovers.'

'How long, Alex? How long do you give this . . . this affair?'

Dear Reader

The background in which a novel is set can be very important to a reader's enjoyment of the story. What type of background do you most enjoy? Do you like a story set in a large international city or do you prefer your story to be set in a quiet rural village away from the hustle and bustle of everyday life? What about exotic locations with hot climates and steamy lifestyles? Let us know and we'll do all we can to get you the story you want!

The Editor

Vanessa Grant began writing her first romance when she was twelve years old. The novel foundered on page fifty, but Vanessa never forgot the magic of having a love story come to life. Although she went on to become an accountant and a college instructor, she never stopped writing and in 1985 her first Mills & Boon novel was published. Vanessa and her husband live in a log home in the forest on one of British Columbia's Gulf Islands.

Recent titles by the same author:

WHEN LOVE RETURNS
HIDDEN MEMORIES
CATALINA'S LOVER

NOTHING LESS THAN LOVE

BY

VANESSA GRANT

MILLS & BOON LIMITED
ETON HOUSE   18-24 PARADISE ROAD
RICHMOND   SURREY   TW9 1SR

for Bobby
in memory of a long-ago day care centre

First published in Great Britain 1992
by Mills & Boon Limited

© Vanessa Grant 1992

Australian copyright 1992
Philippine copyright 1992
This edition 1992

ISBN 0 263 77727 8

Set in Times Roman 10 on 11½ pt.
01-9209-55291 C

Made and printed in Great Britain

CHAPTER ONE

'MAY have to turn back!' the pilot shouted over the engine noise.

'Can't you give it a try?' Sarah squinted to see through the windscreen and wished herself back in her Vancouver office. Anywhere but up here in the remote north, flying through a snowstorm! Her lined trench coat had seemed appropriate in Vancouver, but now she was looking at an incredible blinding blizzard!

The pilot had the kind of ageing toughness that inspired confidence, a leather face that frowned easily, eyes that laughed. Sarah hadn't hesitated to step into his miniature flying machine back in Prince George, but now she wished she'd taken a taxi into Prince George and found a hotel room to wait out the storm instead of continuing her journey.

'Can't you give it a try?' she shouted again to the pilot, knowing that if he couldn't land she would be delayed an extra day. She hadn't time for another day.

Aunt Lori might have problems, but back at the hotel Sarah had her own hassles, all of them urgent. The chef and the *maître d'* were feuding. The only lift that went all the way to the penthouse was giving problems that no one could diagnose. The new booking clerk had double-booked the banquet-room—once for the wedding reception of a timber millionaire's daughter, and again for the dentists' convention the same weekend.

In the four years since her father's plane crash Sarah had learned to delegate all sorts of things. Legal hassles went to Justin Rule, the hotel's lawyer, financial details to the accountant. Sarah herself had more than enough to do looking after the problems that would not delegate, not to mention her mother and her brother. And Aunt Lori.

Aunt Lori's latest problem was a legal one, but it would have been useless to send the dry, practical Justin to deal with her. Sarah wrapped her arms more tightly around her chest and wondered what on earth had possessed Aunt Lori to settle up here. She would have some weird reason for it, of course. Sarah stared through the window of the little bush plane, but she couldn't see anything at all. White and more white. Snow.

The place was fit for Eskimos. No one else.

When Aunt Lori telephoned the day before, Sarah had been sitting behind her big walnut desk. She had reached for the intercom automatically when it buzzed.

'Your aunt,' Brenda's quiet, discreet voice had announced. 'On line two. She's very upset.'

'Excuse me a moment, Warren,' Sarah had murmured.

'Sarah? Is that you?' Lori's voice had sounded frail through the telephone line.

'Yes, Aunt Lori. How are you?'

Through her window Sarah had seen the dismal grey of Vancouver's January sky. In the comfortable chair on the other side of her desk her accountant had been asking the interminable questions that always came when he was preparing year-end financial statements. On the other side of the mahogany door that closed out the rest of the hotel Brenda was waiting with the morning mail and a handful of new complications. And, on the telephone, Aunt Lori.

'Oh, my dear...Sarah, I—I need your help.'

'Aunt Lori?' Sarah leaned forward in her leather chair. Was her aunt actually crying? A hiccup. She *was* crying.

'I—I've been evicted.'

Ever since Uncle Axel died four years ago his widow had been meandering around the continent in the camper-van she and Axel had bought for holidays. Sarah's mother had been furious at her middle-aged sister-in-law behaving like a gypsy, but Sarah had refused to interfere. If Lori was happy, why not leave her be? Then, last year, Lori had inexplicably stopped and rented an apartment in a tiny community in British Columbia's northern interior.

'In the bushes, for God's sake!' Sarah's mother had wailed, but privately Sarah thought Aunt Lori was better off away from Vancouver. Northerners might take a more tolerant view of her eccentricities. Sarah had never been into British Columbia's wild interior before, but she'd had a hazy picture of lumberjacks and miners, rough-spoken pioneer women and a live-and-let-live atmosphere.

'There she is!' the pilot shouted.

Sarah couldn't see anything, but the plane banked to the right and she felt fear crawl up her rigid spine. Did the pilot really know what he was doing? Could he see? What if he crashed into the ground?

The pilot was doing things with his hands, motions that meant he was planning to land. Sarah closed her eyes and tried to pretend that everything looked normal out there. Then she felt a bump, then another, and it wasn't a very smooth landing, but when she opened her eyes the leather face was grinning at her.

'Half-hour more and we'd 'a been too late.'

'Too late?' she repeated faintly.

He was twisting a dial on his radio. 'The road. They don't plough every hour in a place like this, you know. Besides, you gotta think about visibility.'

'Road——' She stared through the windscreen. The road they had landed on was more like a back lane, except that there were only trees around, not houses. Just faint, dark evergreens, half visible through the falling snow. Where in God's name was she? It looked like the end of the world. She said uneasily, 'This isn't even a proper runway.'

He muttered a series of numbers and letters into the radio microphone in front of his lips. Someone must have answered, because he said, 'Got a passenger for you. If I don't get out of here quick, I'll be stuck for a week!'

Sarah parted her lips to protest, but the pilot was twisting and turning and backing out of his door, mumbling, 'This *is* the runway, see? Not a road anybody uses. The old Craven place, and the mayor bought that. But there's the hangar over there—Craven's old barn, it was. This is Elizabeth Lake, not Vancouver, see? Lots of fishermen flying around in summer. Hunters in fall. This time of year——' he shrugged expressively '—nothing.'

He closed the door behind him, then he was shouting at her from outside, but she couldn't hear properly through the body of the plane. Sarah stared out and there was nothing at all but barren whiteness. When the door opened beside her she felt snow falling on her face.

'Hop out, lady. I gotta get out o' here before it socks in again.'

'You're going back? To Prince George?'

'Bloody right. It's now or never.'

She stumbled out of the plane, her legs stiff from the flight. Why hadn't she worn trousers instead of the wool skirt that made climbing out of awkward little planes difficult? What kind of a place was this? Was Aunt Lori actually here? Was anyone here?

She shouted uneasily, 'You're sure this is Elizabeth Lake?'

'Don't worry! He'll be along for you soon!' The pilot deposited Sarah's leather case at her feet. He was leaving and she felt a desperate need to keep him here. She'd asked him to fly her to this place, but to be left alone with only frozen wasteland around——

'Is it always like this here?' she asked desperately.

'Stand back, eh, so I can turn and get out of here?'

Sarah backed towards the barn that was a hangar. There were two small planes outside it, cloaked in snow and tied down against the wind. Perhaps the mayor owned the planes. As for the town...

She couldn't see anything remotely like a town.

The wind breathed along her exposed face and fingers. She pulled her bare hands up into the sleeves of her coat and wrapped her arms tighter around herself. What if no one came? How far was the town? If she were a child, stranded alone out here with only trees and snow...

She was a woman, almost thirty, and she was *not* going to cry! She watched the little plane turn and taxi away from her, choked back the crazy sob in her throat. The barn. Central heating was probably too much to hope for, but the barn—the hangar—did have walls and a roof.

She couldn't hear anything over the roar of the little plane getting ready to leave, but something made her jerk around. Headlights, moving towards her. Coming from the other direction, not the hangar. She hadn't heard the engine, but it was almost on top of her. The truck was coming fast.

She stumbled back, off the edge of the road, afraid she might be invisible with the snow falling. The truck stopped just as she heard the sound of the plane taking off. It was a big truck with big tyres, several inches of snow on top of its roof, a cloud of warm exhaust rising from it.

The headlights blinded her, then they were gone and she blinked. The truck was a cross between a jeep and a station wagon. It had roll bars and big tyres, the sort of thing rich teenagers loved to drive down Vancouver's streets, big and dark and tough.

Out here, she thought wildly, it belonged.

The man climbing out of the truck was wearing a brown leather coat with a parka hood. He was a big man. Tall and broad. Strong. When he stood erect her first thought was that he belonged, too.

He was brown everywhere. Under the parka hood brown hair flecked with white snow. Brown corduroy trousers below the parka. Brown boots. Brown skin— the bit that was uncovered—so maybe the sun shone up here occasionally.

Sarah was not accustomed to feeling the need for a strong man but she was painfully glad he had come. Suddenly alone with only trees and snow around, she had felt horribly vulnerable.

'Who the hell are you?' he demanded. She tensed, because the harshness in his voice was somehow unexpected.

'I——' Why should she explain herself to a stranger? She made her voice stiff, like her body. 'Have you come to take me into Elizabeth Lake?'

His eyes weren't brown. They were grey, suspicious and analytical. She felt him studying her. Her leather city boots. Belted coat. Carefully waving blonde hair caught back from her face in the style that her hairdresser did for her every morning. Sarah knew the image she projected. Attractive. Efficient. In control.

Strangely, his examination made her feel self-conscious.

'What the devil are you doing here?' he demanded grimly.

She wanted to snap back, but habit kept her voice neutral. 'If you're the man my pilot called, I believe you're supposed to take me to Elizabeth Lake. I'm Sarah Stellers.'

'Planning on swimming?' he suggested with quiet mockery. She could see what must be the lake behind him. A smooth expanse of ice.

'The city,' she snapped. 'I want to go into the city. I'll pay you, of course.'

'That's reassuring.' His lips were twitching as he repeated, 'The *city?*' His amusement had warm undertones, like his curling brown hair.

She felt heat crawling up her neck towards her face. 'I'll walk.'

'In those boots?' He swept her with a look that missed nothing. 'I'll take you. Hop in.'

The seat was a long way up. Sarah grabbed on to the door-handle and levered herself up. She pulled the door shut and immediately felt a warm blast of air from the heater. She felt herself relaxing then, soaking up the wonderful heat.

Then she heard the sound behind her.

Heavy breathing.

She spun around in the seat, twisting to see past the head-rest. A dog. A very large dog. Part German Shepherd, she decided uneasily, part something else. The dog must have been lying down in the back seat, but now it was standing, moving towards her.

Sarah's hand fumbled for the door-catch.

'Listen, dog,' she said uneasily, 'just stay there. I'm no threat, and you . . .'

The dog's head cocked to one side. He had his mouth open, tongue hanging out, eyes fixed firmly on her face. Surely the man who owned this truck wouldn't tell her to get in with a vicious dog? All the same——

At the back, the tailgate opened with a screaming metal sound. The dog's head swung.

'Casey, lie down!'

The dog immediately dropped down on the back seat.

The brown man was putting her suitcase in. He must have a name, but he hadn't given it to her. The knowledge that she had climbed into the truck and left him to look after her case made her feel at a disadvantage. He wasn't the kind of man anyone took for granted. Habit, she told herself, frowning uneasily. She lived in a world of doormen and porters.

The dog was watching her from the back with intent eyes. She heard the tailgate close and murmured soothingly, 'It's OK, Casey.' The dog didn't wag his tail or stop watching her, but at least he didn't growl.

Casey's owner climbed in behind the steering-wheel, gave Sarah a hard look, then reached for the controls on the dashboard. Cheerful soul, she thought wryly. Then she felt the warmth flowing on to her legs increase. He had turned up the heater control.

'Thank you,' she managed. She thought he shrugged, but it was hard to tell under that leather coat. Inside the truck he seemed even larger than she had thought.

'Open the glove compartment. There's a pair of mittens in there.'

He was turning the wipers on to clear away the dusting of snow, settling back against the seat as if he always drove relaxed. She reached to open the glove compartment, but she felt stiff and awkward; her fingers would not obey her instructions.

He leaned across and she jerked back, but there was no room to get away. She stared at the broad brown leather shoulder in front of her eyes as he snapped the little door open, pulled out a pair of leather mittens and dropped them in her lap.

'Are you crazy, dressing like that in the middle of winter?' His voice was a growl. 'You could die of exposure out here.'

'Where I come from this *is* winter clothing.' She put her hands into the soft insides of the mittens, curling her fingers into the soft fleece.

'Where? Vancouver? Victoria? Don't you realise we get real winters up here?'

She snapped back, 'I realise it now. This isn't exactly your tourist season, is it?'

He chuckled and she relaxed a little. Her legs felt beautifully warm now, and these thick mittens would protect her hands when she got out.

Behind them the dog made a noise like a groan as he shifted position on the back seat.

Sarah thought she could see shapes up ahead. Buildings. As he drove closer the shapes resolved themselves into houses with snowy, steep roofs, evergreen trees towering over them. Like a Christmas postcard, she thought. He pulled the truck to a stop on a wide street with houses on both sides and a big pile of snow dividing the road into two white ribbons.

'This is Elizabeth Lake. Do you just want to jump out, Sarah Stellers? Or do you have somewhere special you want to go?' He turned towards her and she made herself control the inexplicable reflex that had her pulling back against the door. He said, 'The hotel's closed, by the way. The owners have gone to Hawaii for a holiday.'

'I can understand why,' she said wryly. She could feel her imprisoned hair working its way loose from the knot at the back of her head, the strands tickling against her cheek.

He grinned then and his face lost the harshness. 'We don't get too many tourists in January. Do you have somewhere to go? Were you planning on the hotel?' His eyes had turned speculative and she wondered if he actually thought she was crazy enough to come up here for a holiday in mid-winter.

'I'm going to fourteen Cory Lane,' she said coolly. 'But I can walk, if you'll point the way.'

'I'll take you.' All the good humour drained out of his face. He shoved the truck into gear and repeated, 'Fourteen Cory Lane? You're sure?'

'That's right.' Was there something funny about that address? Trust Aunt Lori to pick it, if that was the case. Probably the local red-light district.

He turned left around a big pile of snow in the middle of the road. 'You wouldn't be visiting Jake McCulloch, I suppose?'

'No,' she agreed. 'I wouldn't.' A minute ago, when he'd smiled at her, she might have told him she'd come to visit her aunt, but now she wasn't volunteering any information. If all northerners were like this, shifting from friendly to surly in a flash, she couldn't imagine what the attraction was for Aunt Lori.

He growled, 'I didn't think so,' and the dog growled too. Then the man turned left and right and the truck pulled up in the drive of a big old house.

The man got out of the driver's side. Sarah opened her door and scrambled down on to the snow. When she got to the back of his truck he was already there. He handed out her case.

'Are you sure this is it? It's supposed to be an apartment.' This house was a rambling old manor house.

'I'm sure.' He had hold of her case and for a moment they both gripped it while he frowned down at her. The grey of his eyes was lit with bits of fire that must be gold flecks. He was frowning again, studying her grimly, then he released the case abruptly in the instant when she'd decided to try to pull it away from him. He growled,

'I'll be seeing you, Sarah Stellers,' and turned away from her without waiting for her answer.

'How much do I owe you?'

'Nothing.' He didn't turn back to look at her, just said, 'Consider it a welcome present from the town.'

'You represent the town, do you?'

'Sometimes,' he agreed.

'Thanks for the ride,' she said stiffly. If he heard, there was no sign. He was climbing into the truck, saying something to the dog inside. Then he was gone, the truck puffing white breath out the back as it roared away along the white street.

Disturbing man, but he was right about the building. The rambling house had been divided into apartments. The front door had four buzzers, but it wasn't locked. Sarah went into the foyer. Inside she found a wide hardwood staircase with a mahogany banister leading upwards. A chandelier hung overhead, welcoming strangers with shafts of light split into colours by prisms. There was a bench that must be old mahogany, meant for sitting on and taking off winter boots. Sarah thought a dealer could get a good start on an antique store with what was here in this foyer. That antique coat-rack. The little love-seat. The mirror on the wall, framed in elaborately carved hardwood.

She scrubbed her boots on the mat and decided they were clear of snow. She didn't fancy stripping them off, prowling around looking for Aunt Lori in her tights. She found Lori's door upstairs at the back, raised her hand to knock and realised that she was still wearing the big leather mittens that the brown man had given her. She would have to get them back to him somehow.

She hesitated before knocking. Twenty-four hours, she promised herself. She would settle Lori's problem in twenty-four hours, then she'd get out of this snowed-in northern community and back where she belonged. She had a mountain of work waiting for her. The brown man was absolutely wrong. He would *not* be seeing her again. She would send the mittens back to him, or have Lori give them to him, or...

She hadn't a clue who he was. No name, although there couldn't be many men like him in a place this size. Big and brown and radiating a strong self-confidence that didn't give a damn what anyone else thought. She shivered as she remembered the way his eyes had taken their survey of her.

Who the hell are you?

Alex Candon couldn't believe he'd actually said those words. He could hear his own voice echoing, flat and harsh and accusing. No wonder she'd looked so startled.

He had driven out to the runway expecting to find himself picking up one of the locals, someone who had managed to fly home ahead of the snowstorm. Jerry, he'd expected, because he knew Jerry Dent was expected back from his Mexican holiday some time this week.

Then his headlights had drawn someone completely unexpected out of the falling snow. A woman, dressed for the city. Tall, blonde, the kind of woman he'd expected to see back in Toronto, not up here. Beautiful in a tailored way that didn't go with the north or the cool softness of falling snow. Cool eyes.

It was the eyes that had done it, because he had the oddest feeling that he recognised the eyes, and that was insane. And yet, all through that short ride, he'd been haunted by the conviction that she felt the same unnerving awareness of him, although her eyes had shown him only ice and efficiency.

Except once, when he'd caught the oddest flash of soft vulnerability. He wouldn't be surprised if he woke up dreaming that look in her eyes.

Sarah Stellers. And she wasn't visiting old Jake, so she must have come to see Lorraine Rooney. He frowned. He was fed up to the teeth with the Rooney woman. She'd turned up in a camper-van last year, had sold the Winnebego to the Dutchsons and moved into his Cory Lane building. For the first couple of months Alex had thought he had a quiet, slightly befuddled middle-aged lady in there—someone who wasn't going to cause him any problem at all.

Alex resisted the impulse to slam on the brakes in front of the little town office. The sooner he got rid of Mrs Lorraine Rooney, the better. If the woman who called herself Sarah Stellers had come to straighten his nutty tenant out, he couldn't be more pleased. As for the strong urge he felt to just keep driving, to keep her inside his truck, take her home and...

He made an angry sound that had Casey snapping his head up with a bark.

'Nothing, Casey. Settle down!'

Nothing at all. Just an aberration caused by the long nights of winter. Probably a sign that he should take a southern holiday somewhere.

'Bill called,' Mary Anne announced as Alex came through the door.

Mary Anne was forty, a cheerful blonde woman who knew everybody in Elizabeth Lake, who had never lost anything in that filing cabinet of hers. Alex figured that she could have run the town herself, but she was paid to be the town secretary half-time, and Alex's office help the other half. She kept her finger on everything to do with the town, but she always deferred to Alex for decisions when he was around.

Being mayor of Elizabeth Lake wasn't exactly a full-time position. If it were, Alex would never have let them talk him into standing for election.

Elizabeth Lake was a hell of a change from Toronto's financial district. In his opinion the best thing about Elizabeth Lake was the fact that it was isolated, small and slow. He'd been away a long time, but when he came back three years ago he'd still known almost everybody in town. It was that kind of place. A man could be mayor, landlord, minor hockey coach, and still have time to smell the flowers or enjoy the warmth radiating from his own fireplace as the flames flickered.

'What's Bill's problem?' Alex asked as he held the door for Casey. Once Casey was inside he closed the door firmly and started stripping off his parka, gloves and boots while the dog stood watching, panting slightly.

Mary Anne said, 'Snow-plough broke down,' and Alex grimaced. The town had only one snow-plough.

'Who flew in?' Mary Anne asked. She'd been dying with curiosity ever since Alex went out to the airstrip.

'A stranger.' Mary Anne would know soon enough, so he added, 'City woman. Yuppie type. She's visiting the Cory Lane place.'

'*Your* Cory Lane place?' Mary Anne speculated eagerly, 'Do you think she's come about Mrs Rooney?'

He nodded grimly. Mrs Lorraine Rooney was working on driving him mad. It wasn't that he minded having to remind her that the rent was due. She always paid in the end and Alex figured that she wasn't the type to have a good business head. But she was causing problems, stirring people up.

Last week she had fixed those amber eyes on him and smiled. 'Why don't you let me read your tea-leaves, Alexander Owen Candon?'

A bunch of nonsense, although he had no idea how she'd learned his middle name. He grinned now, remembering that smile. She'd go over well in a circus, with those weird clothes and those eyes.

Only, damn it, she'd created chaos in this little town with her quiet trouble-making. Alex Candon was accustomed to being in control. He was damned if a fruitcake middle-aged weirdo was going to run crazy circles around him. And if she'd pulled in that sleek, gorgeous blonde from the big city to help in her battle it wasn't going to make any difference.

Alex sat down in his big leather chair and let a lazy collection of odds and ends consume his attention for the next two hours. There was no point in going out, because Sarah Stellers would be here soon. He closed his eyes and her image was there, strong and clear. She was tall, blonde, gorgeous in a downplayed, elegant way. Definitely *not* his type, but he might as well wait for her, get it over with.

She had been his type of woman once. Back in the Toronto days.

A woman like Denise.

The dog sprawled at his feet made a sound between a grumble and a growl, bringing Alex back from a time and a place that was firmly in his past. He picked up the telephone, made several calls in connection with the disabled snow-plough, then called the principal of the local school to discuss cancelling school tomorrow.

'I'm gone for the day,' announced Mary Anne suddenly, smiling up from her desk. Outside it was already dark.

'See you tomorrow,' he said absently. 'Say hello to Blake for me. And watch yourself out there. Slippery streets.'

Alone in the little office, Alex punched in his access codes on the computer. The computer at the Toronto brokerage on the other side of the country considered for a second, then allowed Alex access. Alex scanned the transactions for the stocks he was interested in, then placed two buy orders and four sell. Then he added another buy order, purely on instinct. He'd learned to trust his instincts when it came to the market.

When the knock came on the door he knew it would be Sarah. Her name suggested a woman who would be soft and gentle inside, but she had a businesslike knock.

'Come!' he called as he keyed in the command to log off the data service. Then he swung around his big swivel chair to watch her coming through the door.

Under the coat she had long, slender, model's legs. The wind and snow hadn't done her hair any good. The smooth, complex knot at the back must be losing control. There was a cloud of blonde silky stuff trailing around her face, giving her a soft look that wasn't reflected in her hazel eyes.

Her eyes widened as she recognised him. He saw anger there, but she controlled it at once. Alex found himself wondering what would happen in her eyes if he freed her hair. He thought it would tumble around her face in rich waves that begged a man to bury his fingers in the wildness.

'I told you I'd see you,' he said softly.

He decided that she was accustomed to controlling her emotions, but he wondered if she might be all woman underneath, soft and hot, if she let herself loose. He frowned and pushed his hand through his hair, turning it into even greater disarray, fighting a ridiculously graphic fantasy of Sarah Stellers with all the control gone.

'You're Mr Candon?' she demanded in a flat voice.

'Alex,' he corrected idly, wondering what it would take to get through that tension she drew around herself like a blanket.

'You gave Lorraine Rooney an eviction order.'

'That's right.' Could he talk her into dinner tonight? The eyes, that imprisoned hair trying to get free. The way her mouth turned down slightly.

It would be stupid to reach for her, because he knew her type. Toronto's financial district was full of women like her. Denise had been one of them. Independent, competent, something in her eyes that said she was accustomed to giving orders. Not the kind of woman who could give him what he had come to understand he needed out of life.

No, but...

She was still shivering, trying to hide it because it would look like a weakness. She had discarded the mittens he'd given her earlier, probably because they didn't fit the business image that she projected.

She seemed to have finished assessing him. Her voice was brisk, announcing, 'I'm Mrs Rooney's niece. She's asked me to represent her against you.'

Against. Their eyes met. Hers held impatience. He wondered what she saw in his. He said implacably, 'She violated the terms of her lease.'

She had probably come on a fast trip, planning a one-day turn-around. It was in her eyes. She wanted to get back to the big city as quickly as possible. Alex thought it would be a hell of a good thing for his peace of mind if she left, and soon.

So why the hell was he thinking of ways to keep her here? He didn't want a woman like this in his life, no matter what fantasies she stirred.

Sarah Stellers had eyes a man could drown in if he found the key.

CHAPTER TWO

SARAH had come into this office expecting to find some growling, embittered landowner who wanted her aunt out so that he could raise the rent for another tenant. But, whatever the landlord's motive in ejecting Aunt Lori, the last thing Sarah had expected was the brown man from the truck, his grey eyes watching her with that disconcerting intensity, his dog lifting his head and thumping the long tail on the rug.

He demanded, 'Can you make her behave?'

'Behave? What's she—what are you alleging she's done?' Alleging. A good word, she decided. Not admitting anything. Sarah kept her face blank as her father's admonitions echoed in her mind. 'Don't ever help the opposition state a complaint. Don't give anything away unless you gain something by the move.'

What on earth had Aunt Lori got herself into this time?

He asked, 'Didn't she show you the eviction letter?'

'She couldn't find it.' Her aunt had been lying, of course. Lori's dedication to truth was erratic at best.

His eyes narrowed under thick, dark brows, but amazingly he smiled. 'This could take a while, then. Do you want a cup of coffee?' He waved towards the pot standing on top of a filing cabinet.

'Decaff?' she asked warily.

'No, the real stuff.'

'Then no, thanks.' She would have loved a coffee, but she had trouble enough sleeping with the hotel hassles that always kept her awake hours after work should be

22

over. She didn't need to add potent caffeine when the sun had already set.

'Then why don't we discuss your aunt's situation over dinner?'

She felt her jaw going rigid. 'You can't throw an old lady out on the street in the dead of winter.' The dog's head jerked towards Sarah at the sound of her anger.

'She's not exactly in her dotage,' he said mildly, 'but no, of course I won't throw her out if she has nowhere to go. But she's not destitute. She sold that Winnebego for twenty thousand last summer. She hasn't spent that here, I can assure you, and she hasn't gone anywhere.'

How on earth did he know details of Aunt Lori's personal finances? Sarah's lips parted in protest, but he went on in a cool voice, 'If she won't go, I'll have to start action against her in court, and I can assure you I'd win.'

She snapped, 'You know the judge, I suppose?' and was shocked at her own implication.

He didn't react at all, just sat in that big leather chair, relaxed as if nothing she said inconvenienced him in the least. He had said earlier that he represented the town, but now she suspected that it was the other way around—that the townspeople did what this man told them to do.

She moved restlessly, aware of the long masculine legs stretched out towards her, of his eyes and that feeling that he could move suddenly and without any effort at all. She loosened the belt of her coat because she was suddenly too warm. She found herself staring at his legs, his feet in leather shoes that he must have changed into since he picked her up. She watched him reach one foot towards the dog to scratch. Casey thumped his tail while Sarah's own legs felt crazily weak.

Then his eyes narrowed, watching her, and she had the ridiculous conviction that he knew exactly what she was feeling. She stammered, 'What—what on earth has she done to you? Aunt Lori is—she's harmless, for heaven's sake.'

There were lines on either side of his broad mouth. Laughter-lines, surely, because he was not a man who worried a lot. He sounded amused, not impatient, as he told her, 'She's a disaster, your innocent aunt. Believe me, it may take a while, but if she won't behave I'll get rid of her.' Her lips parted on a protest and he added softly, 'On the other hand, you and I could discuss ways to make her behave.'

Making Aunt Lori behave was pretty unlikely, but Sarah made her own mouth a hard line and asked, 'What are you accusing her of?'

'I'll tell you over dinner. I don't imagine it's the first time you've had to get your aunt out of a mess, but why not eat first?'

'Mr Candon——'

'Alex,' he corrected. 'I can offer you burning logs in the fireplace, and your chair close to the warmth.'

'Why?' Instinctively she knew that this was a man who always had reasons for the decisions he made.

'After the trip you must have had today I can't, in good conscience, start laying more problems on you until I've fed you, at the very least. After all, Elizabeth Lake has a reputation for hospitality. And I can offer you a warm fire, good food.'

She'd been offered bribes in her time—money from customers who wanted a room when there was none, tickets to a sold-out concert. This was the first time she'd been offered food and a fire. Her lips twitched and the amusement gurgled in her voice. 'This must be some restaurant.' Her father's voice echoed somewhere in her mind. 'Don't let him charm you. Keep cool, keep in control.'

'My place,' he said. 'Not a restaurant.'

His place, and he hadn't said it with any suggestive overtones, but, for a second, in her imagination... images... his hand tracing the cool curve of her cheek, sending shivers everywhere as he kept her eyes locked with his...masculine lips, a hard mouth softening as it came down to possess.

No!

Sarah felt her face flaming. She turned abruptly to stare at a painting of a lake surrounded by an autumn-gold forest. Behind her the dog scrambled to his feet.

'Lie down, Casey.'

She licked her lips and asked, without turning her head to look at him, 'Is this what your lake looks like in autumn?'

'That's right.'

It wasn't his voice making her tremble, but the strangeness inside herself. What on earth had happened to send images crawling along her nerves to make her heart shudder and her face colour like a young girl's? Maybe it was the man—not that she—— Simply because he was so big and tough and at home in this harsh place.

When she looked at him he was smiling. His face changed completely with his laughter. 'The dog will be on good behaviour,' he promised. 'Casey's nothing but a softie.'

Casey's big tail swept the floor at the sound of his name. Sarah eyed the giant dog. 'A softie?' she speculated disbelievingly. 'Like his master?'

Whatever Alex Candon was, he was no softie. Master and dog were both big and strong and a little frightening. With the dog, Sarah understood why she felt nervous. Those teeth. As for the man—well, it must be something to do with this place. She was accustomed to her own world surrounding her safely when she encountered men. Accustomed to Brenda in the next office, or to a room full of restaurant guests. Not a man saying, 'My place,' and promising his dog's good behaviour, but not his own. Heaven knew how long it had been since she had been completely alone in a building with a man, especially a stranger.

Not since Kevin, she thought, and suddenly the memory of Kevin turned sharp and fresh in her mind.

'How about it?' Elizabeth Lake's mayor asked. 'Relax before business? You look as if you've had quite a day.'

'I have.'

'So how about dinner?'

Sarah spent her life dealing with people, many of them difficult. She recognised the message behind his words. Letting Alex Candon give her dinner was probably the only way to settle Aunt Lori's situation and get her out of here by tomorrow. What harm could it do to let him give her food and warmth? He was the mayor of this little town, so the townspeople must trust him.

'All right,' she agreed, but she saw something flash in his eyes and decided that she would be wary. 'Don't trust anyone,' her father had always said, and he could easily have been talking about a man like this, who wore a lazy mask over calculating eyes.

Alex turned to push keys on the console of the computer behind him. Sarah recognised the computer. Top of the range. Expensive. Definitely out of place in this little village where they didn't even have a proper airport. The man didn't belong here, either, not really. He had power hidden under those lazy eyes. When he stood up she stepped back because he was even bigger than she remembered.

'I still have your leather mittens,' she said, needing something to say, to cover the nervousness that his towering nearness sent trembling in her chest. 'They're at Aunt Lori's.'

Her aunt's beautiful apartment actually belonged to this man, and if Sarah didn't find some way to avert the eviction order Aunt Lori would be out—not on the street, but unhappy and confused and hurt.

'Wear them,' he suggested. His chin was narrowed, thrust out by nature, a sign that he could be stubborn when he wanted. 'When you leave put them on the desk in the foyer of your aunt's place. Do you mind if we make a stop on the way to my place?'

'A stop?' She tried to control the nervousness in her voice.

He turned and looked at her as if he could see right through the coat. She stared back uneasily. Grey eyes were disconcerting. They didn't give much away. When he finally turned away from her and opened the door she went out to his truck feeling as if she had escaped some inexplicable danger.

If she ever came to this place again she would bring a big parka like his, and the kind of boots they called mukluks, with fur inside and outside. Thank heavens his truck had a good heater!

They sat together in the moving truck in silence, without words, but oddly without tension either. Alex Candon was no ordinary backwoods man. He had the brawny muscle which she might associate with a logging-faller, but she kept glimpsing something else under the smooth exterior of the man. Something in the eyes, in the way his expression carefully gave nothing away. The way he watched her when he thought she wasn't looking. He made her shiver with apprehension. That's what it was. Apprehension.

He drove to a snow-bound car park in front of a small grocery store. He didn't pull his truck up beside the other cars and trucks outside the building. Instead he drove on into the deep snow.

'You'll get stuck,' she worried, then wished the words unsaid when he flashed her an amused glance.

'The truck is in four-wheel drive,' he explained.

'I should have known,' she muttered. Snow and ice and the need to thrust the beast into four-wheel drive. He laughed as if he could see her thoughts and she wondered if his laugh would still surprise her when she knew him better.

Why would she ever come to know him better? She was leaving tomorrow.

There was a snow-plough standing in the middle of the uncleared section. Alex pulled up beside another truck, bigger and older than his, its headlights playing on the snow-covered plough. Sarah saw a short man and a tall man, both dressed in heavy parkas, standing in the beam of the headlights, bent over something on the plough.

Alex rolled his window down to call, 'Bill! How does it look?'

The tall man came over to lean against the side of the truck. 'Bloody day it picked to break down,' he grumbled to Alex.

Sarah found her gaze fixed on the hair at the back of Alex's head, the way it curled down until it tangled in the pushed-back hood of his parka.

'What do you think?' asked Alex.

'She's got problems.' The men gestured towards the plough. 'Joe says we need parts from Smithers to fix it. Want to have a look?'

Alex glanced at Sarah. 'I'll just be a minute.'

'All in a day's work?' She realised that she was smiling.

'That's right,' he agreed. 'I'll leave the heater on.'

When he was outside with the other two men Sarah glanced at Casey, who was standing on the back seat, his nose pushed against the window. Luckily the animal didn't seem to bite. They were warm together, she and the dog, with the heater working so well that Sarah rolled her own window down a bit.

She smiled, imagining her mother's reaction to this scene. Jane Stellers's idea of going to dinner with the mayor would definitely not include stopping to look at an ailing snow-plough. Although, if Aunt Lori were here, *she* would be out there with the men, looking at the engine, having no idea what she was seeing but giving advice anyway.

Sarah had more sense than her aunt. The truck was warm and secure, beautiful heat flowing over her legs and hands... She satisfied herself with the window cracked down and curious ears listening. The bigger man was about Alex's height. They grew them big in the north, she decided with a smile, and the parkas added even more bulk. Alex was saying something about the valves and the small man said maybe it needed a ring job. Alex said something about an old engine and why didn't Burt have a look, just in case he could jury-rig something until they could get parts?

The tall man said something about school and Alex must have agreed, because they all nodded. Then Alex was back, opening the door and jumping in quickly, almost as if he wanted to preserve the warmth for her.

'Is it the only snow-plough?' she asked as he pulled out of the car park. He nodded and she worried, 'What if you can't fix it?'

'We'll work it out.'

'How?'

His mouth quirked up at the corner. 'Get people to put snow-blades on their trucks, form a work party.'

'Oh.' She would like to see that, a dozen trucks working their way along the roads of this little town, men with parkas and boots and warm smiles. 'Can you put a plough on this truck?' He nodded and she asked abruptly, 'Do you live out by that airstrip?'

She had an image of some shadowy house near that barn that was a hangar. They would be the only two people in the world, out there. Disconcerting, and she should never have accepted his invitation. Although perhaps there was a Mrs Mayor and maybe even children.

He shifted down and turned to go up a hill, so they weren't going out to the airstrip. Up ahead Sarah could see a station wagon sitting on the road, tracks behind it and none ahead. She said, 'The pilot said the mayor had bought the property out at the airstrip, made the barn into a hangar. I thought you might live out there with the hangar and the airplanes.'

He shifted down and pulled on to the wrong side of the road to pass the abandoned car slowly. 'You're already picking up local gossip. Stick around and you'll know all about us.'

She made some sound of agreement, but she wasn't hanging around a place like this. She twisted to look back, but the abandoned car was only a shadow thrown by the streetlight.

'He lives beside me,' Alex told her. 'He couldn't make it up the hill with the fresh snow.'

'Shouldn't a tow-truck——'

'Simpler to wait until the road's ploughed. The car's not in the way until the road's clear again.'

It had not been in his way. He'd just geared down and driven around it. How many cars were regularly abandoned in the middle of the road when the plough couldn't keep up with the fresh falling snow? She thought of Vancouver and the chaos that ensued on the rare occasion when snow fell heavily in the inner city. Chaos, but the cars that got stuck were promptly towed away.

'It's like another world.' She didn't realise she had spoken aloud until he threw her another of those amused glances. 'Do you have a telephone at your place?' she asked abruptly.

'Yes. Running water, too.'

'I didn't—I just meant——' She flushed, knowing she was behaving as awkwardly as a young girl. 'I've got to call my aunt. Let her know where I am.'

His face shuttered, reminding her that he wasn't a friend. He was Aunt Lori's enemy, the man who had served the eviction notice.

When he pulled up in front of his own garage Sarah twisted and she could see the lights of the town. His house was on top of the hill above the little town. Maybe two or three hundred houses down there, and she wasn't sure which one was the old renovated home that had become Aunt Lori's accommodation.

He turned the engine off and opened his own door, letting Casey out, then coming around to let Sarah out and explain, 'Normally I could deliver you under cover in the garage, but I can't get the garage door open until I plough the drive.' He said it casually, as if everyone ploughed snow out of his or her front drive. She could see the imposing profile of the cedar home perched here on top of the hill. This was a new home. If he could pay for it he could easily hire someone to do his drive. A completely different lifestyle from anything she was accustomed to, because she suspected that he would enjoy ploughing the drive out, fixing the snow-blade on his truck and moving mountains of snow.

Casey's ears perked up and he made a pleading noise in his throat. Alex dropped his hand to the dog's head. 'OK, boy. Go ahead.' Instantly Casey was tearing off

through the snow, heading over a snow-bank and dis-
appearing downhill.

'My brother lives down the hill,' Alex explained.
'Casey must have heard Kelly—my nephew. They're great
pals. Actually, Casey is supposed to be Kelly's dog.'

'Oh? He seems very much your dog.'

'My sister-in-law,' he explained with a grin, 'turns out
to be allergic to dogs. She's been bothered by problems
for years, but she never had the allergy tests done until
recently.'

'So you inherited Casey.' She followed him up wide,
curving stairs that might have a rock garden flowing on
either side when spring came. Everything was white
now—even the footsteps he must have left that morning
filled in with fresh snow. There was a light burning over
a varnished door with a stained-glass insert, but it was
dark inside, as if no one was home.

Sarah was expecting him to pull out a key, but he
opened an invisible little door on the outer wall and
punched in a code on the little number-pad inside. She
heard a click that must have been the lock, and he pushed
the door open. She dropped her eyes as she stepped
inside, felt the warmth of him even through her coat and
his parka as she passed through the door he was holding.
So much for thinking this was the back of beyond. In
his office, he had the same computer that she had in the
hotel, and lord knew what other high-tech stuff there
was in this beautiful house.

'How old is Kelly?' she asked.

Alex switched on the light inside and she drew in a
sharp breath, overwhelmed by the abundance of warmth.
Varnished cedar walls. A big, graceful archway drawing
her on towards the thickly carpeted living-room.
Paintings over the fireplace. She stepped forward, drawn
to them, then stopped, realising that she was leaving

melting snow on the carpet as she moved. When she turned back she saw that the light outside the front door shafted in through the stained-glass window insert, making magic on the walls and the white ceiling, the colours all blending together with warmth.

He said, 'Seventeen.'

She whispered, 'You must have paid your decorator a fortune for this,' then flushed because she'd been brought up not to make comments like that.

He was watching her, not looking at the walls and furniture. 'I'm happy with it,' he said simply.

She remembered the colours in the painting on the wall of his office. 'It must be marvellous in spring, with all the colours outside, golds and reds shafting in through that stained glass with the sun.'

'Why don't you shed your coat and boots? I'll get a fire going.'

She moved around the perimeter of the living-room in her stockinged feet while he bent to the fireplace. His carpet was soft and luxurious underfoot, warm. He had shed his parka and she was warm even without her coat, but she couldn't see any sign of radiators or vents, which meant that the house also had the newest heating system, with heated floors and ceilings. She could make a guess as to what it cost to build a house like this. Hadn't they added twenty new rooms to the hotel last year? None of this was cheap, and Alex Candon was turning into a mystery she was determined not to ask about. Maybe he'd won a lottery, or... well, something that brought in more money than being mayor of a little place with a population of around a thousand.

He stood up from the crackling fire and gestured to a big easy chair close to the fire, then moved to the built-in stereo system on the wall where he touched two buttons to make music flow into the room.

'Relax, Sarah, and I'll do something about dinner.'

'I—thanks.' She felt self-conscious with his eyes on her, aware of her stockinged feet and the vulnerability she felt. She picked up a magazine on the small glass table beside the chair, sat down glancing at it, turning the pages and trying not to feel him watching. She felt so strange, as if she were trapped inside a warm nest with Alex Candon, and there wasn't another soul in the world.

It must be hunger causing this feeling of unreality, of waiting.

She felt tension rising until he left the room, then she sagged into the chair, drained as if from some physical contest of strength. Was he actually cooking her supper? She could feel the quietness of this sprawling hill-top house and knew that they were completely alone here. She turned the pages of the magazine, glancing idly at the pictures, her feet bathing in the radiant warmth from the fire. She turned another page. AN EXECUTIVE GUIDE TO THE BEST IN TOKYO. She chuckled.

'What's funny?'

She jerked upright in the easy chair and flipped the magazine shut, but he wasn't there, just his voice from back through that archway. 'I'm reading your *Financial Post*. All about the best in Tokyo for the visiting executive.'

She thought he laughed, then he was coming through the archway and there was a smile in his grey eyes. He had a wine glass in his hand and he brought it to her. When their fingers touched she felt a shock that made a breathless sound escape her throat.

'Thanks,' she said hastily, lifting the glass to mask her confusion. 'Have you been to Tokyo?'

'As it happens, yes.'

'Tokyo's a world away from here.' She frowned up at him. 'You're a mystery man, Alex. You don't fit here.' His brows went up and she flushed, then his gaze flowed to her face, telling her that he was aware of the strange effect he had on her.

'I belong,' he said quietly. 'About dinner—you're not vegetarian, are you? I might have a problem if you limit your diet to tofu and vegetables.'

'Whatever you cook will taste great to me.' She bit her lip, hearing the breathless quality in her own voice. She stood up abruptly. 'Can I help?'

'No. Just relax, put your feet up.'

She stepped back as he moved towards her, losing her balance and sitting down in the chair abruptly, awkwardly. He leaned over to push the lever on the side of the chair, throwing the recliner back and taking her with it. She gasped and clung to her glass with both hands to stop herself from reaching out to touch the breadth of his chest. She could feel the heat from his body, could smell the tang of the aftershave he used. She felt her head spinning as, for just a second, his dark form blocked out her light. Then he stepped back. She hoped her gasp sounded like surprise at being tipped back, not shocking awareness of a man's nearness.

'I could have done that myself!' Her voice was tense and breathless.

'You always do things for yourself, don't you, Sarah?'

She frowned at the soft note of censure in his voice. There was no one she turned to personally for little gestures of warmth and caring. She didn't know how he knew that, except that it might be written in her face after four years in control of the legacy her father had left behind. She raised her glass again and sipped on the wine, wishing he would stop watching her. She had the uncomfortable feeling that he knew she had been called the ice princess of Vancouver's hospitality industry, that she had lost the only man she'd ever tried to love because she didn't have time or space in her life for luxuries like love.

'I should call Aunt Lori,' she said uneasily. She had forgotten, as if nothing existed but this place and . . . and this man.

'I called her.'

'You—what did she say?'

He shrugged and Sarah decided that he had probably been brisk and casual, just giving the message that Sarah would be delayed and not stopping for comments.

'Why did you call? I could have——'

'You're tired.'

She pushed back a wisp of hair that was tickling her ear and wondered if this was part of his tactic to soften her up before he persuaded her to take Aunt Lori away. She found herself explaining, 'The jet from Vancouver was supposed to land at Smithers. I had a rental car booked there, planned to drive here and have transportation.' Transportation to chase around looking for the evil landlord, she thought with a smile. 'We spent two hours in the air. It was supposed to be a fifty-minute flight, but we kept dodging from airport to airport, arriving with the snow every time, unable to land. We ended up in Prince George, and I had to charter a bush plane to get here.'

He nodded. 'Flying up here in winter, you can land anywhere. I don't suppose it was a very smooth flight.'

'No, but I don't get airsick.' Terrified was more like it, she thought, remembering the aborted landing back at the Smithers airport when the pilot decided at the last minute that he didn't have enough visibility. He'd apologised to the passengers over the intercom, and they had shrugged as if it were a daily occurrence, but Sarah's heart had been hammering from the shock of that bang and the sound of the jets blasting away as if desperate to get away from the ground. 'Next time,' she said briskly, 'I'm going to come dressed right, and I'll check the snow predictions before I get on the jet.'

'Do that,' he urged. 'Wear a good coat, and boots with warmth in them.'

'And mittens,' she added, though there would not be a next time, and if it happened she would buy gloves that matched her bag and boots, not suede mittens with thick sheepskin linings.

'So relax,' he commanded, moving back through that archway that must lead towards his kitchen.

'What are you going to feed me?'

When he turned back to answer she realised that she had spoken for only one reason. To stop him from going away. She pushed her hair back and her fingers got caught in the part of her hairdo that hadn't yet come loose. 'Anything will do,' she added hastily. 'And your fire is lovely.'

'We're having moose stew.'

'Moose? As in big animals with lots of horns?'

'That's the one.' He smiled and her lips curved to answer.

'Is it good?'

'Very.'

She was smiling when he left to go back into the kitchen. Very good, and he was probably a good cook. A good something else, too, because something had to pay for this house. It certainly wouldn't be the allotment that a tiny town council made to the mayor of Elizabeth Lake.

She picked up the *Financial Post* again, but none of it seemed to matter much at the moment. How on earth did you cook moose? She enjoyed cooking and would

have liked to follow him out to his kitchen, to watch.
She seldom had freedom in a kitchen, but right now she
should be looking for his telephone, using the time before
dinner to contact the hotel and talk to Brenda, who
would be somewhere in the hotel, available if Sarah
called.

She wriggled her toes and felt the warmth crawling up
her legs. Nice, and she liked the music he'd chosen. She
didn't recognise it. Something classical, but her edu-
cation had neglected that sort of thing, concentrating on
business and management and taking over the hotel,
although when Mike grew up he'd been supposed to come
in with her, share management. For a few years she had
continued to hope that her brother would join her and
share the burden, but that would never happen now.
Once she had believed that she could be free of the place
entirely, but she'd been very young then. Young and full
of dreams and freshly in love with Kevin Drew.

She knew now that it was her task forever, managing
the family hotel and keeping track of the crises that
turned up in the lives of the family. Sarah closed her
eyes tighter, feeling the tension through her whole body.
Restlessness, that's what it was. She needed to be back,
looking after things. In the last four years the only holidays she'd taken were working ones, looking at other
hotels, making notes to keep competitive. But there
wasn't even a hotel open in Elizabeth Lake right now,
so she couldn't find even the pale shadow of competition to evaluate.

For a little while, here in Alex Candon's home, she
was effectively incommunicado. Brenda had Aunt Lori's
number. She would give it to Warren or Justin if they
needed it, but Sarah would be very surprised if any of
them could communicate successfully about business to
Aunt Lori. That was exactly the reason Sarah had come

on this crazy mission herself. To rescue Aunt Lori from the man in the kitchen, because nobody could manage a straight conversation with Lorraine Rooney, so Justin would be useless. Justin was great when it came to law and negotiations, but hopeless dealing with Aunt Lori.

Of course, that was why she was here enjoying this fire, but first she would relax a little, and if the hotel burned down... well, she'd be free then, wouldn't she? She smiled, letting her eyes close, feeling the warmth of the room and the music and the fire radiating towards her feet. She knew it was fantasy, that a fire in the hotel wouldn't free her. Stellers Gardens was insured. Hotels could be rebuilt and her inheritance and her family were her albatross forever.

But if she was stuck here in this chair, idle, she could pretend for just a little while.

CHAPTER THREE

'MORE?' Alex asked.

'Hmmm. Yes, please.' Sarah leaned back to allow him to refill her bowl. 'Don't tell me you whipped this up while I was lazing in front of your fireplace?' The rich moose stew was delicious, the big pieces of home-style bread irresistible.

He shook his head. 'It was in the freezer, and I can't take credit for cooking it either.'

Who? she wondered. If she asked it would sound as if she were interested in him as a man. She wasn't, but she couldn't help speculating why a man so obviously eligible should appear to be living alone. Her boots were in the cupboard with a pair of men's hiking boots and two pairs of men's dress shoes. No sign of women's shoes or boots, no woman's coat hanging with her too-thin trench coat.

She lifted her spoon and breathed in the delicious aroma. No, there was no woman living with Alex. The magazines in the living-room were financial and technical, not one woman's magazine. The glimpse she'd had of the kitchen had revealed it as gleaming and bare, modern and almost sterile. He probably had a housekeeper who came in to sterilise the place. Sarah shook her head slightly and flushed at the question in his eyes.

'What do you do in Vancouver, Sarah?'

'Work.' She did not want to talk about hotels. Not here, with quiet all around. 'What about you? What do you do in Elizabeth Lake besides mayoring?'

'This and that.' He leaned forward as she pushed her bowl away. 'Finished with that?'

'Yes, thanks. It was great.' Her voice was stilted. He would think she was crazy if she admitted that she hadn't had a date with a man in years. 'I'll do the dishes,' she offered awkwardly.

'There's a dishwasher.'

Just as well, she thought wryly. It wasn't a date. She didn't have dates, not any more, and she couldn't remember when she had done dishes. The Monday dinners at her mother's were the closest she came to a private kitchen.

Uncomfortable with her awareness of this disturbing man, Sarah moved restlessly away from the table. She went into the living-room. It was a softer room than the kitchen, warm with the flicker of lazy flames over the logs in his fireplace.

She called back to him, 'What exactly did Aunt Lori do to get herself evicted?'

'Drove me nuts,' he answered, and she couldn't help grinning at that, although of course it wasn't funny that Aunt Lori was in danger of losing her home.

Sarah held her breath as Alex followed her to the living room. He leaned against the hearth, pushing his hands into his pockets in a way that seemed to emphasise the breadth of his shoulders under the brown sweater he wore. His eyes were narrowed, studying her.

Self-consciously, she pushed back the wisp of hair that had escaped again. There was music coming from the stereo. The speakers must be hidden, but the soft music flowed everywhere. She wondered what his arms would feel like around her. She felt her eyes drooping, almost as if he were moving with her to the music, his fingers spread out possessively on her back.

'Dance?' he asked.

'No!' she gasped, her eyes flying wide. Surely he couldn't actually *see* her thoughts?

'Why don't you let your hair down?'

'Literally, you mean?' her voice squeaked. 'Or figuratively?'

'Both.'

This wasn't a joke. She was feeling very strange tonight. There was a strange wildness in her blood. She would have to be very, very careful, or she might just move towards him, reach out her hand and...

She crossed her arms, holding her elbows in the palms of her hands. 'I could take an example from you,' she suggested tightly. 'You're an open book, of course.' How had they got into this kind of fencing? 'Aunt Lori?' she reminded him. 'I'm here because you evicted my aunt.'

'I'm *trying* to evict her,' he corrected.

'But why?'

When he moved she tensed as if he had touched her.

'Relax,' he murmured as he wandered over to the big built-in bookcase nearer the stereo. She had to force herself to keep still, but he was completely relaxed as he asked lazily, 'Do you have any idea how many teenage girls there are in Elizabeth Lake?'

'What is this? Demographics?' She made her hands fall to her side, but they felt awkward. She didn't know what to do with her hands, as if she were suffering through the first time she had to get up in front of everybody and make a speech.

'No,' he said absently. 'Not demographics. I'm talking about your aunt.'

'Aunt Lori and teenagers?' She was confused.

He did not seem to move, but he was facing her now, watching her. His gaze did something uncomfortable to her breathing. 'Fourteen teenage girls. They all travel on the school bus together, out to Smithers for high school.

Fourteen angry mothers—fifteen, if you count Ellie Sandahls. I haven't talked to Ellie yet, so we can't count her.'

'Of course not.' Sarah felt like laughing because there was frustrated laughter in his eyes.

'Do you know what she's been doing?'

'Giving them advice?' He nodded and she shook her head warily. 'What's wrong with that? Aunt Lori's advice is usually...' Radical, she thought uneasily. Wasn't it Lori who had told Sarah to throw everything over and walk away with Kevin? Lori who had said, 'Don't take the hotel administration degree, it's not right for you.'

'What's wrong is that their mothers don't like it. And they expect me to do something about it.' He moved then and under his calm she could feel raw energy. He was too big. Sarah wished she had kept her high-heeled boots on, but she didn't realise that she had backed away from him until his eyes narrowed.

'You say she violated her lease?' She stared into the fire to mask her discomfort. 'Do you expect me to believe that she signed a clause that forbids giving advice?'

'No. One agreeing not to run a business on my property.'

'A business!' She ran her fingers along the hearth, concentrating on the warmth from the fire, on the stones that had been laid into the fireplace surround. Anything to keep from looking at heavy brows lowered over inscrutable grey eyes. 'I'm sure she's not charging teenagers for advice.'

'She keeps putting a sign out, hanging it out her window: "Tea-leaf readings—advice about love and life." Whenever I ask her to take it down she does, but the next day it's back. And Delaney Smith gave her twenty dollars to read her teacup and tell her whether or not to marry Austin Newley.'

'Just how old is this Smith girl?'

'Forty-five,' he admitted.

Sarah couldn't stop a grin. She thought his eyes were smiling too. 'Hardly a teenager. And is the wedding on or off?'

He brushed that away as irrelevant. 'Lorraine Rooney rented an apartment from me, not an office. Come to that, she doesn't have a business licence, which makes the whole operation illegal in any case. If she wants to start a business she should find appropriate premises.'

'Appropriate?' She bit her lip but could not suppress a chuckle. 'A tea-shop, perhaps?'

He smiled, but he wasn't giving way. 'If you've come up here to do something about this, get her to stop running a business on my premises.'

'OK. I'll talk to her.' Sarah tried to look positive, but Aunt Lori could be terribly stubborn.

'How long have you allocated to that job?'

'What do you mean?'

He shrugged. 'You didn't come up here for a holiday with your aunt. You came to solve her problems, but you've got the rat race written all over you. Before you ever got here you decided just how long you could stay.'

Twenty-four hours, but he made it sound as if Aunt Lori's importance could be measured in hours and minutes, relationships put into time management. That reminded her uncomfortably of Kevin and she snapped, 'Could I see a copy of the lease?' His brows went up and she explained, 'Aunt Lori misplaced her copy.'

He laughed. 'She should look in her teacup to find it, then.'

Sarah felt her jaw clenching with tension. 'If you refuse to provide me with a copy, I'll turn the whole thing over to my lawyer.' She was making a mess of this. Keep it cool, her father had always counselled. She swallowed and said, 'You can hardly evict my aunt on the basis of a lease that you won't produce.'

'I'll drop the lease by for you tomorrow.' She wasn't sure if it was scornful amusement or anger in his eyes. 'Tell your lawyer that if Lorraine Rooney stops using my premises for retail services she can stay.' There wasn't any laziness in his voice now. It was flat and deliberate and he said, 'But I'll need that promise in writing.'

She wished her skirt had pockets. She needed somewhere to bury her hands, to hide the irrational trembling. She took a deep breath. Handing this over to Justin would be a disaster. The only solution was to persuade Alex Candon to soften his position, or Lori to give up reading tea-leaves, but Aunt Lori was virtually uncontrollable.

She managed to say stiffly, 'I'll pick the lease up at your office, then. First thing tomorrow morning. I'll be leaving tomorrow. And could you give me a copy of the eviction order?'

'She's lost that, too?'

'Misplaced.'

'Of course. Will you be able to persuade her to behave?'

Behave. As if Aunt Lori were a child. Sarah said coldly, 'I'll be getting my lawyer's opinion on the lease.'

'Do that, but remember there's ten days to run on that eviction order, and I'll be taking action on the eleventh day.'

A few minutes ago this had seemed like something they could settle between them. His grey eyes had seemed warm and friendly, amused by Aunt Lori's idiosyncrasies—although Sarah hadn't thought he would change his mind about demanding a change. She was the one who had brought lawyers into it, and now his eyes were grey ice.

She moved uneasily towards the archway to the foyer. 'I think it's time I left.'

'You're probably right.' He got her coat out of the cupboard, then put on his own parka.

'I can walk; it's only a few blocks,' she told him.

He ignored her and put on his boots. She had come up to Elizabeth Lake feeling competent and businesslike, but somehow he'd made her feel uncertain and uneasy. She wasn't sure how he'd done it, but she was uncomfortably aware that it might have been deliberate.

She felt the crisp night on her face as soon as she went through the door. She tightened the belt on her coat, as if that could turn winter into the warmth back there in Alex's living-room.

The drive down to Cory Lane took about three minutes. To Sarah it seemed endless. She made awkward conversation, asking, 'How many people *are* there in Elizabeth Lake?'

'About a thousand.' He didn't even glance at her as he answered.

'Are there more in summer?'

'A few.'

She stretched her legs towards the warmth from the heater vent on the floor. 'Have you lived here long?'

'Yes.'

She grimaced and managed to bite her tongue on ten other questions. He didn't fit any image she had ever had of sleepy northern towns. She wondered about him, but his answers weren't telling her anything. No more than she'd told him when he asked where she came from, what she did in Vancouver.

Strangers. That's what they were. Strangers who didn't really trust each other enough to share the superficial details of their life. She bit her lip and watched the darkened houses on either side of the road. Snow-covered roofs. Lighted windows, lighted porches. Footsteps through the snow and snow falling in a thick blanket.

He pulled to a stop and she got out quickly, climbing down to the snow-covered pavement. Someone had shovelled the path outside Aunt Lori's. It couldn't have been Alex because he had been with her ever since she left to tackle him in his office.

'Thanks for the supper,' she said politely. He shrugged and she added, 'I'll pick up the lease in the morning.'

'Don't rush.' He had one leather-gloved hand on the gear-lever, the other curled around the wheel, telling her without words that he would rather be driving away than talking to her. 'There's no hurry. You're not getting out of here tomorrow.'

She rammed her hands into her pockets. 'What makes you sure I won't leave tomorrow? Have you taken up telling people's futures?' She bit her lip, realising that her voice was rising, echoing over the quiet street. 'I'll be gone by noon. Tomorrow.'

His eyes might be telling her something, but his face was a dark mask inside the truck. 'Sarah Stellers, I'd take a bet on your being here this time tomorrow. Just name your stakes.'

'You're on,' she snapped. 'But you'll lose.'

'I doubt that.' He *was* laughing at her. She ground her teeth together at the confidence in his voice. 'Prepare to pay up, Sarah. Meanwhile, close the door so I can get out of here.'

She slammed it and stomped up the path towards the lighted front door. He hadn't driven away yet. She grabbed the rail and got up the stairs without looking back at him. She would look a fool if she was stopped at the front door for lack of a key, but luckily the door swung open and she found herself inside with the barrier shut. Why had he stayed, watching her? To make sure

she got inside safely? Not likely. This was tiny Elizabeth
Lake with all of a thousand people, according to its
mayor. The biggest danger a woman would incur walking
the streets at night would be——

Perhaps bears coming down from the big hill to the
north. She was probably in the middle of bear country.
Wolves, too, and she might wake up tonight to the sound
of their howling. That would be a change from her telephone ringing at three a.m. to announce that some
businessman was threatening to call the police because
of the banging noise coming from the next room.

Sarah tried the knob to Aunt Lori's apartment.
Luckily that door was open, too. She slipped into the
apartment quietly, surprised to find lights shining everywhere. It was a lovely apartment. This building must
have been decorated by the same person who had done
Alex's house.

If Aunt Lori left the lights on all night and utilities
were included in the rent, Alex Candon would have
another legitimate complaint against his tenant. Sarah
went through the little foyer, through the living-room
with its spectacular view. She glanced at her watch, but
the face was blank, as if time had ceased. It felt late,
the sky outside black. Lori didn't use this living-room
much, although it was attractively furnished with a deep,
comfortable sofa and chairs. Whose furniture? Had Lori
rented the place furnished? Sarah frowned and followed
the lighted path from the living-room into the corridor.

The door to the guest-bedroom was open and the light
was on there, too. In Lori's bedroom brightness illumi-
nated a mess of bedclothes, tumbled everywhere. No sign
of Lori. The bathroom light was on—another empty
room.

Lori's soft voice came twisting out from the only room that didn't have bright light streaming from it. 'Sarah? In here, dear!'

Sarah opened the door to the study and stepped in. Here the light was dim, masked by a thin piece of fabric draped over the lamp. There was a big desk in the room, but Lori had pushed it against the wall and covered it with the paraphernalia that she took everywhere. An assortment of romance novels, old photograph albums, and the knitting that Sarah remembered as a constant companion to Lori.

Her aunt was in a low chair by the window. The curtains weren't drawn. From down below, her silhouette might look like a witch's. Sarah moved to the window and let the blind down with a bang.

'Did you have a nice time, dear?'

'It wasn't a date, Aunt Lori. It was a business dinner, to talk about your eviction order.' She flushed, remembering the way Alex's grey eyes had watched her. She sat down across from her aunt. 'Aunt Lori, we have to talk.'

Lori smiled the vague smile that Sarah remembered so well. 'Dear, don't worry about it. What did you have for dinner?'

'Moose stew.'

Lori smiled with satisfaction. 'Very good.'

Sarah leaned forward. 'Aunt Lori...an eviction order isn't something you can ignore. You must know that. We have to talk about it.'

Lori smiled again. 'Don't worry, dear. Go to bed and we'll talk in the morning. You'll need a good rest, you know. And do watch out for those boots.'

'Boots——?' Sarah's gaze moved restlessly to her feet. 'All right,' she agreed, knowing she wasn't fit tonight to take on her aunt's slippery notions of conversation.

'But first thing in the morning we have to have a serious talk.' She lifted her wrist again, but the face of her watch was still blank. 'What time is it?'

'Time?' said Lori cryptically. 'Don't sweat the little things, dear.'

'Little things like time?' Time ruled her life. There was never enough for all the things that needed to be done.

'That's right,' said Aunt Lori agreeably. 'Now go to bed and get a good sleep. He is a nice man, isn't he?'

'Nice!' Sarah laughed unwillingly. 'He's trying to evict you!'

Her aunt shrugged. 'You'll look after that, dear. I know you will. Now don't forget about the boots.'

In the guest bedroom Sarah slipped out of her skirt and sweater, bra and tights. She quickly slipped on her jersey nightgown and got under the quilt. Crazy, she thought, closing her eyes, feeling the world spinning as if her long day were still surging around her. Crazy for Aunt Lori to send her to bed as if she were a girl. Lori, who thought time was a little thing, who forgot to pay her bills because bank accounts were boring.

Sarah had never needed anyone to look after her. Her father had always said that she was born efficient. It was what she was best at.

She was almost asleep when she realised that Alex hadn't mentioned the stakes of their bet. Well, no matter. Whatever the stakes, she was not going to lose.

It was dark when Sarah woke, and quiet. She lay motionless for a moment, feeling the differences. No muted hum from the lifts, no sounds from the traffic below her hotel-room window. What time was it? She got up and dressed quickly, then went looking for a clock.

The light was on in the study that was Aunt Lori's favourite room, but the room was empty. Sarah had no idea when her aunt had gone to bed. She had a vague memory of waking once with moonlight streaming through the window and hearing something like music, from somewhere. In the moonlight the bedroom where she slept had seemed strangely magical, all breathless silhouettes.

The whole building was dead quiet, but Sarah's mental clock said it was time to get up. She couldn't find a clock in the quiet, walk-through kitchen, or in the living-room. There was no television, either, although she hadn't thought television was one of the things that Aunt Lori didn't believe in. She finally found a radio in the living-room and turned it on low. The announcer told her cheerfully that the weather was a record-breaker.

'Crews are working all over the area, trying to get the roads clear. Until they do, here's a list of school closures in the district.' He read a long list that included Elizabeth Lake Elementary School.

The joys of living in the north, thought Sarah with a quiet laugh, but it was hard to believe in harsh winter when she was sitting in the warm security of Aunt Lori's apartment.

'Coming up to ten minutes after eight,' the announcer finally told her.

It was still dark outside.

She toasted two pieces of stale bread and spread on jam from a jar that looked like home preserves. Had Aunt Lori started bottling her own jam? Not likely. She had probably traded jam for a look at the tea-leaves. Sarah was going to have to talk to Lori about the teen-agers. About charging money.

There was a note stuck on to the refrigerator door with a ragged piece of Scotch tape.

Don't worry, Sarah. Worry is such a waste of energy. Trust Aunt Lori!

Sarah got out her slim briefcase and started making a list. Then, in the quiet of the rising sun, she went through the notes she'd brought with her and used her little recorder to record three business letters for Brenda, her assistant, to type when she got back. By that time it was late enough for the telephone, but when she picked up the receiver to dial she heard only silence. She clicked the button again and again, then checked the wall-jack, but found nothing obvious wrong.

The telephone must have worked last night when Alex called Aunt Lori, but it was dead now. She prowled the room in quiet frustration. Every morning she started her day with a light breakfast in her room while she jotted down the day's priority list. Then, right after breakfast, she started clearing up business on the telephone.

She certainly wasn't going to wait all morning for Lori to get up and look blank when Sarah told her the phone was out of order. There must be a telephone *somewhere!* She hadn't noticed one in the foyer the night before, but she went out now to check anyway.

No telephone there, but when she peered out through the window-pane beside the front door she spotted the familiar shape of a telephone-booth down at the corner. Outside.

She went back to put on her boots. The leather was stiff on her feet, still damp from the snow that had melted on them. She should have thought to put them somewhere where they could dry overnight. Alex Candon would laugh because he would know that she wasn't accustomed to wet boots. She lived an indoor existence. Years ago she'd gone skiing and hiking, but there was never time now. And here—well, it was a different life-style, that was all.

The snow started to fall again as she made her way down the slippery path and across the street. She licked a snowflake off her upper lip while she waited for Justin to answer his phone. It tasted cool and fresh.

When Justin answered he wasn't particularly helpful. 'If it's written in the lease that way, you haven't a leg to stand on,' he said reasonably.

'Well, can't you think of some way around it?'

She could hear his shrug. He had more important things to do than worry about a scatty middle-aged woman who liked to look into teacups. The only reason he was bothering was because the Stellers Gardens Hotel was one of his biggest clients, so it was good business to do a personal favour for Sarah.

'She could move,' he suggested. 'Or give the owner a promise in writing; that seems reasonable. Word it carefully to comply without unduly restricting her private—ah—freedoms. I can draft it for you, but I should see the lease first. Why don't you fax it to me?'

'I don't know if there's a fax service here.' Sarah sighed. 'And, anyway, I don't think she would give the promise. And she doesn't want to move.'

Anyone but Justin would sound irritated, but he simply said, 'It's one or the other, always assuming he's telling the truth about the lease. You must instruct your aunt to take better care of her valuable papers. As for what you can do—the only other option is to buy the place, which seems excessive. She's not all that stable, is she? If you did buy the property your aunt could decide to move next summer and you'd be stuck with a block of apartments in the middle of nowhere.'

Was that the answer? Would Alex sell?

Why not, if the price was right? The family corporation could buy it. Four apartment units in the house, and they all appeared to be occupied. It must be feasible as a revenue property. She'd have to check it out, of course, but, if Alex was agreeable in principle, why not?

'Better to give the owner what he wants,' concluded Justin. 'It sounds reasonable enough.'

'Thanks for the advice, Justin. I'll be back this afternoon—well, by tonight, anyway. We'll talk about it then.'

Sarah hung up and made notes on her little pad. Get the copy of the lease, then wake up Aunt Lori and talk to her. Alex said she was running a business. Well, Lori could agree not to engage in any commercial enterprise. Commercial meant money. Alex might not like it if she kept on reading tea-leaves for free, but what could he do? He'd have no grounds to kick Lori out if she wasn't making any money out of her teatime activities.

She heard the engine as she came out of the telephone-booth and her heart lost track of its rhythm even before she swung around to look. Alex! She had known it was him. She tried to push the door to the booth shut, but it jammed on the snow at the bottom.

He rolled his window down. 'What are you up to?' he asked, his breath white on the air. 'Sneaking out in the early morning to use a pay-phone? Secret conversations?'

She felt her lips answering his smile. 'No, I wouldn't need to. Aunt Lori's still asleep.' Lori had been up half the night with her knitting, had been in the kitchen boiling a kettle when Sarah drifted off to sleep. For tea, probably, but she wasn't telling Alex that. 'Her phone's out of order. You didn't get it disconnected, did you?'

'Why would I do that?'

'I don't know.'

It was a crazy accusation and he was grinning as he said, 'I'm the mayor, and I play around with old buildings and a bit of stock-market stuff on the side. None of it gives me power with giants like BC Tel. If you want, I'll report the line out of service for you.'

'I already phoned it in.'

He nodded. 'Of course you did. Hop in. I'm going to my office and I'll get you a copy of that lease.' She hesitated and he said, 'Shake the snow off before you get in, otherwise it'll melt and get you wet.'

She stood on the road brushing off her shoulders and the white carpet over her arms, shaking her hair and seeing the cloud of white all around herself. Like a child, she thought, and she was frowning when she climbed into the passenger-seat.

'I could get hold of a decent winter coat and boots for you,' he offered.

'I'm not exactly a charity case.'

He glanced at her. 'No, you're a well-heeled lady executive.'

She frowned because it made it sound a bad thing to be, although his voice was neutral as he added, 'But you're dressed for a coastal winter, and you might have noticed we don't have a clothing store here in Elizabeth Lake. My sister-in-law's about your size, and you'd be welcome to borrow some suitable gear.'

'I'm leaving today,' she reminded him. 'I *am* leaving, and we didn't name the stakes on our bet last night.'

He pulled the truck to a stop outside the little town office. The sign on the building said, 'Town of Elizabeth Lake', but the letters were coated with the falling snow and she wouldn't have been able to read if she hadn't seen it the day before. He shut the engine off, but made no move to release his seatbelt. She turned towards him and felt shock when their gazes met. She had always thought of grey eyes as cool.

'Well, Sarah? What stakes do you suggest for our wager?'

Their wager. Her father had always said that only fools gambled, but Sarah could see the image of herself in a game of chance with Alex. Playing poker. His grey eyes staring at her over the five cards in his hand. A shark. She touched her dry, chapped lips with her tongue. That was crazy. Of course he wasn't a shark, not up here in this little place.

'If I win—how about if you withdraw Aunt Lori's eviction order?' She wasn't sure why she felt such a pressure of tension in her chest. She knew that he would laugh at her suggestion, then maybe they would bet five dollars on her transportation out of here.

She watched him turn towards her, one arm up the back of the seat and his leather-covered hand only inches from her shoulder. She stared at his glove and fought down the breathless fantasy of Alex slipping the glove off before he reached to touch her with long, sensitive fingers.

He said quietly, 'All right. Aunt Lori's eviction.'

'You're not serious?' It had been a joke, a challenge thrown out. She had expected his lips to twitch with silent laughter, but he wasn't smiling, not frowning, just watching with calculation behind narrowed eyes. She repeated, 'Are you serious?'

'Why not? If you win, your flakey aunt can stay. The teenagers' mothers can look out for themselves.' His slow smile made her uneasy. 'If you lose...'

'If I lose?' The shudder in her chest took her by surprise. She should be feeling as if she were winning already, because this bet would free her to leave immediately. Just by making the wager he would be en-

'Not on those terms! It's stupid—I—I'll be out of here today.' She turned to find the door-handle. 'There's nothing you can——'

His fingers tangled in her hair and she jerked around, facing him, unable then to pull her eyes away from his as he said reasonably, 'Then why not take the gamble?'

'Because . . . because——' She realised that she was chewing on the corner of her lower lip, forced her teeth to release their hold. He'd taken his glove off. When had he done that? His fingers were still in her hair, but hair wasn't supposed to have nerves. She gulped and whispered, 'Because I'm not a gambler.'

'Too bad.' He moved back, freeing her to breathe as his hand left her hair. She watched as he raked his long fingers through his own hair, turning the brown waves to unruly curls that were faintly damp.

Why was his hair wet? From melting snow? Had he stood out in the falling whiteness, scraping his windscreen while snow fell on his head? Or was the dampness from his morning shower?

His shower. Alex with his head thrown back as the water flowed over his face. Broad, naked shoulders. When he turned off the water there would be drops of water clinging to the curling hair that would be on his chest. A towel around his waist, or perhaps——

She jerked her head forward, stared at the fine layer of snow that had already blanketed the windscreen. She had to stop this! She'd been overworking. That was it. She'd spent the last few years working every waking hour. This was the first time she'd been forced to idleness. All the things she had been missing were surging up and—— It wasn't the man. Not Alex specifically, except that he'd made this outrageous suggestion and her mind—— She hadn't realised it, but she must be moving into one of those adult life crises, suddenly missing the things she didn't have, the things she'd had to turn away from years ago.

'Well, Sarah?'

'I——' She swallowed a dry lump in her throat. 'You're not serious? Of course you're not.' He must be trying to shock her, although she wouldn't have expected that of him. 'You're *not* serious, are you?'

'I wouldn't back out on a wager.'

She didn't dare look at him, although his voice sounded as if his lips were smiling. She almost laughed except that suddenly she *did* look, and his eyes weren't warm. They were flat and calculating, the grey turned to cold slate so that she asked warily, 'Do you gamble often?'

'Yes. And, in fairness, I should warn you that I usually win.'

'You can't call it gambling if you normally win.' He meant the stock market, of course. Hadn't he said that he played the market? She whispered, 'But you'd lose this time, so you're lucky I'm not taking you up on it. But—what harm would there be to just stop persecuting Aunt Lori anyway?'

'Persecuting?' He was amused. 'I assure you, I'm the one who's being persecuted. Come answer my telephone one day and you'll see what I mean. Irate mothers are no joke.' He pushed his door open. 'Are you coming in?'

She followed him into the office and murmured something polite when he introduced her to a middle-aged secretary, a woman with unlikely blonde hair and a loose sweatshirt draped over ample proportions.

'You flew in yesterday?' asked Mary Anne. 'First visit?'

'Yes,' Sarah agreed stiffly.

Alex said, 'Mary Anne, get the Rooney correspondence and the lease, would you? I'd like copies.'

Mary Anne pushed her wheeled secretary's chair across the office, stopped in front of a low filing cabinet and pulled open a drawer as she announced, 'Bill called and said with the snow-plough down they'd better cancel minor hockey Saturday afternoon. The principal says what about Monday, could you let him know? And your dad wants to know what's the score if he has to do a medevac for Judy Swill? And coffee's made.' She pulled a file out and pinned Sarah with her curious eyes. 'You want a coffee?'

'No, thanks.' Sarah managed to keep her lips from twitching. Mary Anne was definitely rough-and-ready in her style, but she'd found the file right away and she was at the copy machine while Alex poured a cup of coffee and raised his brows to Sarah.

'Sure you don't want some?'

She shook her head. 'I have to go.'

'I'll drive you back.'

She shook her head firmly. 'I can walk.'

By the time she had gone three blocks Sarah wished that she had accepted Alex's offer of a ride. The snow was deeper now, drifting around her ankles. Her boots did not grip well and the high heels were treacherous.

Sarah dodged her way around a smiling man wielding a snow-shovel.

'Nice day, eh?' he offered.

'Yes,' she agreed, years of habit with customers bringing a smile to her lips. 'It's a beautiful day.'

But, unwillingly, her eyes swept the street ahead. Everything was fresh and white, even the evergreens behind the houses. The clinging white flakes were drifting down everywhere, blanketing the world in bright newness. She found herself humming the notes from the song 'Winter Wonderland' as she walked on.

There was a woman on the corner by the pay-telephone that Sarah had used earlier. She was shovelling her bit of pavement, wearing furry boots and a big scarf wrapped around her head over a thick wool jacket.

'Hi,' she offered cheerfully. 'Nice day, isn't it?'

'Lovely,' agreed Sarah, amazed to discover that she meant it. It was, she realised suddenly, a beautiful day. A beautiful town.

The woman gestured at the pavement, which was now half-clear of snow. 'It would dump snow on us when my husband's away. I really do hate shovelling.' She pushed the shovel in energetically and announced, 'I'm Joyce. Are you visiting Lori Rooney?'

'Yes,' she agreed. Sarah wasn't used to personal questions, but she added awkwardly, 'I'm her niece.'

'Tell her hello from me, will you? And I'll be over for that cup of tea tomorrow.'

Sarah crossed the road to Lori's building, wondering just how many people in Elizabeth Lake had tea with her aunt. And why not, for heavens' sake? Alex Candon had no right to complain.

No right, so long as Lori didn't take money from her guests.

When Sarah came into Lori's apartment her aunt emerged from the kitchen with a big lasagne-pan in her hands. She was wearing jeans with a drifting red smock on top and was barefoot. 'What about pasta?' she demanded.

'Pasta?' Sarah echoed blankly.

'Supper tonight. Do you suppose we should call and invite him?'

'Him? Who is *him?*'

'Alex Candon,' said Lori impatiently.

'I don't believe it!' Sarah bent her head to undo the belt of her coat. 'The man's kicking you out, and you want him to dinner? Did you know your telephone's not working?'

Lori's eyes fogged. 'Did they send me a letter?'

'I imagine they did.' Sarah sighed. 'You didn't pay your bill?'

'It's somewhere around here.' Lori lifted the pan. 'Do you think he likes lasagne?'

'Listen to me, Aunt Lori. He—Alex Candon—wants you to sign a letter agreeing not to run a business out of this apartment.' Lori got that slippery look on her face and Sarah pulled out the papers she'd slipped into her deep coat pocket. She spread them out on the coffee-table and said briskly, 'I talked to Justin, and it's a reasonable request. I can't stay for dinner. I've got to get back to Vancouver. Why don't you find that telephone bill? I'll fix it up for you, get your phone going again. We'll get your bills sent down to me.'

Sarah should have arranged that long ago. Lori had always been scatty about paying bills. It was a wonder she paid her rent, amazing that she wasn't being evicted for non-payment. Sarah frowned and said, 'While you're looking for the phone bill I'll check over this lease.'

Of course it was perfectly plain. Alex contended that Aunt Lori was running a business out of her apartment, and when Sarah called out from the living-room, 'Aunt Lori, have you been taking money from the people who come to talk to you?' her aunt came back in with a big jar of tomato sauce clutched to her breast.

'Sometimes,' she replied with a casual shrug. 'It's never much.'

'You'll have to stop charging if you're going to stay here, Aunt Lori.'

Lori shook her head. 'I don't think I can do that,' she said vaguely.

Sarah recognised that look in Lori's eyes. This was hopeless. 'You could move,' suggested Sarah, dropping the papers and following her aunt into the kitchen, stopping to stare at the mess on the counter. 'What *are* you doing in here? Are you feeding an army?'

'He's a big man,' said Lori calmly. 'He'll have a big appetite.' She was chopping up the remnants of a roast to add to a mountain of onions in the frying-pan. Sarah blinked at the onion fumes as her aunt said, 'I make a good lasagne sauce, you know. It's my best thing.'

'Have you thought of moving somewhere else? Another apartment, or—why not get a storefront somewhere, a tea-shop?'

'Martha Carridon's already got a tea-shop, down the other end of town. And I like it here. It's the best place in the whole town.'

'Another town?' suggested Sarah, but Lori wasn't even listening to that.

Lori pulled open the door of the refrigerator and bent to the crisper compartment. She mumbled something into the vegetables.

'What?' demanded Lori.

'I'll stay right here. You'll look after it, Sarah. You've always succeeded, dear. Except with Kevin.'

Sarah felt completely helpless, a sense of defeat made worse because Aunt Lori had brought Kevin's name into this. She said weakly, 'You're going to have to move.'

Lori plopped the vegetables down on the counter. The celery slid off the pile and fell on to the floor. 'Now, dear, why don't you go somewhere for a while? I've got cooking to do. Don't forget the sweater.'

'Aunt Lori? Why did you call for me to come?' There was no percentage in getting angry with Lori, but she couldn't keep the frustration out of her voice. 'I can't settle this for you if you won't listen to reason. You've got to compromise. Alex Candon does have the law on his side. You'll either have to agree to stop taking money, or move into another place.'

'I couldn't do that. Don't worry, Sarah. It's going to be fine. You'll see.'

Sarah sighed. 'I'm going out to the telephone.'

'Fine, dear.'

Outside the woman with a shovel had worked her way a couple of feet further along the pavement in her shovelling marathon. As Sarah crossed the street she shovelled another scoop of white stuff, throwing it on to a growing pile where her front lawn should be.

The woman asked curiously, 'You're not going to stand out there and phone, are you?'

Sarah nodded. She felt surprisingly warm with the sweater Aunt Lori had given her under her coat, and Alex's leather mittens over her hands. 'My aunt's phone's out of order,' she explained.

'You can use mine.' Joyce waved back towards the house. 'It's in the kitchen. Go ahead. The baby's sleeping, and the dog's in the basement. Just walk in and use it.'

'No, that's fine. I——'

Joyce slid the shovel into a snow-bank. 'You can't stand out here in the snow.' She waved her gloved hand towards the briefcase in Sarah's hands. 'That doesn't look like a short call, and wouldn't you be much more comfortable in my kitchen?'

'I couldn't——'

'Lori's done lots for me. She minds the baby sometimes, and she won't take anything for it. So come on in,' insisted Joyce.

Sarah gave up and followed. 'I'm making a long-distance call,' she said to Joyce's back as they climbed the freshly shovelled stairs to the small house. 'I'll use my calling-card.'

'No problem.' Joyce stomped her boots on the landing and Sarah followed suit, taking her boots off and leaving them on the mat inside with Joyce's.

'There's the phone. And the phone book. And do you want a cup of coffee while you're calling?' Joyce was pouring, taking Sarah's desire for caffeine for granted. 'Take your time, now. I'll be downstairs with the laundry, and there's no hurry at all.'

Sarah called Brenda first. 'I'm planning to be back some time today.'

'Thank goodness!' said her assistant. 'Things are pretty hectic around here.'

'Anything in particular?' Sarah listened to Brenda's problems, her eyes taking in Joyce's cheerful little kitchen. There was a row of baby-bottles on the counter, clean and gleaming. A sprawling green plant with big leaves had taken over the window above the sink. Sarah thought of her own room in the hotel. Elegant. Efficient. Sterile.

Tension, pressures. Brenda's voice evoked that other life. 'The usual crises. Double bookings, a party insisting they had reservations, but it turned out they were booked in the Bayshore. And the chef called in sick. Appendicitis. I called in the temp we used last year, and she says she can give us a week, but then she's going cooking on a big tour boat. She'd rather work in the Caribbean for the winter, she says.'

Sarah sighed and promised, 'I'll be back today, late probably.'

After she said goodbye to Brenda Sarah rummaged through Joyce's telephone book. The yellow pages had charter-plane companies listed for several nearby towns. Sarah called the first one listed for Smithers.

No problem. The plane would come for her at two this afternoon.

She would have been safe taking Alex's stakes.

Joyce came upstairs and poured Sarah another cup of coffee. Sarah glanced at the big clock over her fridge and decided that she could spare ten minutes. 'I left your telephone number with the charter-plane company,' she said. 'I hope you don't mind? Just in case they need to call me back.'

'No problem,' said Joyce, stirring sugar into her own cup. 'I think your aunt's the neatest thing!'

Sarah laughed, thinking that her aunt was neat, all right, but nuts.

She escaped Joyce's friendly gossip after fifteen minutes, then walked directly to Alex's office. She had her hand out to open the door to the town office when he pulled it open from inside. She jerked back and just avoided a collision.

'I see you're wearing the mittens,' he said approvingly.

Her fingers curled inside them. 'Yes, thanks. They are warm. Were you going out?' He nodded and she said quickly, 'I wanted to talk to you.'

'Come with me, then,' he invited.

'Where?'

'The snow-plough, then the local ice arena.' Through the door came the sound of a telephone ringing. 'Let's go, though, before Mary Ann calls me back for that phone.' He took her arm and moved her towards the truck. Another man came past, head lowered against the snow blowing into his face. He glanced at Alex and Sarah with a look of surprise.

She bit her lip and asked Alex, 'Would you consider selling the Cory Lane place?'

His hand had curved to cup her shoulder through her coat, but at her question he stopped and looked down with a frown. 'No, I wouldn't, and you'd be crazy to buy it. You can't manage a rental unit here from the plush office of a Vancouver hotel, and there's no property management service here. You'd have nothing but problems.'

She knew he was right. 'How did you know I worked at a hotel?'

'I asked.' His hand returned to her shoulder, urging her towards the truck.

She went two steps under his guidance, then stopped abruptly. 'Asked who?'

He opened the passenger door of the truck. 'Are you going to get in?'

'Why were you asking questions about me? Who did you ask?'

'Because I wanted to know.'

'Who?'

'Charles Kantos.' He pulled the door wider. 'Are you getting in?'

She moved uneasily closer. She demanded, 'How do you know *him?* Does he come fishing up here?' It didn't sound much like Kantos, unless there was money in a fishing holiday, preferably a lot of money to be made from dealing in land.

'We went to college together.' He was standing at the door to the truck as if he might wait there forever.

Sarah cleared her throat. 'I—if you still want that wager, I'll—I'll take your terms.' His eyes narrowed and she gulped. 'So long as we get the wording clear. Aunt Lori's eviction against a night at your place.' She managed not to look away from his narrowed eyes. '*At* your place,' she repeated stiffly. 'If I do lose, I'm sleeping on your sofa, not in your bed. And I'm sleeping alone.'

His voice was unexpectedly gentle. 'Sarah, I'd never force you into anything you didn't want to do.'

There were other kinds of persuasion than force, but hadn't she proved herself immune? She rammed her hands into her pockets with difficulty. The bulky mittens got in her way. She licked her lips and said uneasily, 'So it's a deal? If I get out of here today, you'll let Aunt Lori stay?'

'It's a deal. And if you're still here tonight you sleep at my place.'

She gave a jerk of her chin, turning away from him. As she climbed into the truck she felt a moment of panic as he closed the door on her.

When he started the engine she asked, 'What made you think I couldn't get out of here today?'

'The snowstorm. The broken-down plough.'

She remembered the flight yesterday, the pilot uncertain that he could land. But the charter company had told her this morning that they were expecting a break in the weather that afternoon, that they were sure they could get a plane in for her.

'That's not going to be enough to stop me,' she said. 'And I could get a ride out, couldn't I?'

'Not likely.' He put the gear into neutral and set the brake, then leaned across in front of her to open the glove compartment. She pulled back into the seat, but his arm pressed into her leg as he got a window-scraper out. 'The road's closed. We've called for help from the highway contractors for snow removal, but they're fighting blizzard conditions through the whole district. They won't get the road clear until Sunday.'

'There are other ways.' If the plane couldn't come Alex would still lose his bet. Joyce had a neighbour with a snowmobile and, according to Joyce, a northerner on a snowmobile could go anywhere there was snow. 'You don't really expect to win, do you, Alex? Is this just a way to let Aunt Lori off the hook?'

He didn't answer, but got out of the truck, leaving the engine running and the heater warming as he scraped the window.

Of course he did not expect to win. A man like Alex Candon didn't have to make wagers to get access to women. And . . . well, it didn't make much sense that he would want her in any case. She knew her own reputation. Four years ago Kevin had accused her of having ice in her heart. Sometimes she thought he was right, because there didn't seem to be anyone in her life who penetrated past the surface. She simply hadn't time for relationships, hadn't had time for Kevin, the man she'd once been engaged to marry. It had hurt, losing him, but the pain had closed over long ago.

Alex got back in and slammed his door shut. He put on the wipers and she watched their sweep keeping the window clear of falling snow.

'Can you let me off at Cory Lane?'

'You don't want to see the plough again?'

She smiled. 'No, thanks. I'm not into snow-ploughs, although I'll admit the thought of riding one appeals to me.' She hadn't meant to say that, and she added quickly, 'I've got to pack.'

A night in his house. He'd promised that he wouldn't use force. She shivered and shook off the crawling panic. She wasn't going to lose, but if she did there would surely be no problem glaring coldly at him and turning any possibility of romance to ice.

'Bye, then,' she said brightly when he stopped at her aunt's place. She got out quickly, before he could, and ran towards the building.

Upstairs she swept into the guest-bedroom and packed her things in a flurry of efficiency. When she was finished she put her suitcase in the corridor, all ready to go, then went to find Aunt Lori.

Lori was slaving in the warm kitchen, making enough lasagne to feed an army despite Sarah's repeated insistence that she was leaving.

'I've worked it out about your eviction,' Sarah told her, 'but you do have to be more discreet. Teenage girls do have mothers, and I know you'd be giving them good advice, and you enjoy company, but you can't go upsetting their parents. And when you read tea-leaves for an adult—well, if they have to pay, couldn't you tell them to give the money to charity?'

Aunt Lori looked thoughtful about that, but the knock on the door came before Sarah could pursue her advantage.

It was Joyce, flushed and breathless. 'The charter company called. They say could you call them back right away.'

From the kitchen Lori called out, 'Sarah! Tell Alex dinner will be ready about six.'

Joyce blinked. 'Is Alex Candon coming to dinner here?' She frowned. 'I didn't know you and he...'

'We're not,' said Sarah firmly. 'He's Aunt Lori's landlord. Can I use your phone to return that call?'

'Of course. Any time. I told you that.' She glanced into the kitchen where Lori was making determined noise, then lowered her voice and asked Sarah, 'She forgot to pay her bill again, didn't she? I should have reminded her, because I saw her open it. She was talking, you see, and she stuffed the bill down into the crack in the big chair. I don't think she even knew she did it.'

Sarah choked back a laugh. Aunt Lori needed a keeper, although she would certainly deny the suggestion herself. 'Just let me get my coat, would you, Joyce?' And the sweater. Sarah was getting used to dressing up for the weather outside. If she were staying she would take Alex up on the offer of his sister's boots.

She wasn't staying.

CHAPTER FIVE

SARAH gripped the telephone receiver tightly. 'Say that again?'

The voice crackled slightly, as if the snow had affected the telephone system, too. 'That runway's in no shape for a landing...contacted... Sorry, but we can't make it.'

'Can't—who did you contact?'

'...Ms Stellers, they say down there that they haven't been able to plough that runway since yesterday morning...half a metre of snow since then, and there's no way we can land without a clear strip. If you've got to get out of there, try the chopper companies, although I've got to warn you we're losing visibility here and I doubt you'll get anything.'

When Sarah called both helicopter charter companies told her, 'Sorry. Not today. Try after the storm's over.'

Outside was all white. Every time she went out the snow was deeper, still falling. She frowned and realised that the only vehicles she'd seen moving around were four-wheel-drive monsters like Alex's truck.

'Joyce, can you introduce me to your friend with the snowmobile?'

Joyce frowned. 'Well...'

Sarah closed her eyes. Damn! She should have known better than to trust someone else. Joyce had been chattering this morning, saying getting out wouldn't be any problem. But now she looked uneasy.

Sarah demanded, 'Who is it? Where does he live? If you've got the phone number, I'll call myself.'

Joyce said, 'I'll call, but...' She dialled and Sarah listened uneasily as Joyce said, 'Harry? I've got a friend here who needs to get out to Smithers today...yes, I—— Well, I wondered about your snowmobile.' Joyce's eyes were on Sarah and she was listening to the voice that came strongly through the telephone. 'Well, no, I don't—— Sarah, have you driven one before?'

Sarah shook her head, knowing that it would be foolish to lie. She wouldn't have a clue what to do with a snowmobile, and she had no idea of the way to Smithers. 'I'll pay him,' she said, and Joyce relayed that offer, but uncomfortably.

'Sorry,' she said when she hung up the phone. 'He says it's pretty late, and he wouldn't be back before dark if he did it. He doesn't like the look of the weather.'

Sarah said, 'That's all right,' although it wasn't, because she didn't know what else she could try to get out of here. Roads closed. No bush plane. No helicopter. The man with a snowmobile wasn't willing to help. 'Do other people have snowmobiles?'

'Well, lots of them, I guess, but—why don't you ask Alex Candon? He's got a helicopter. And I think he must still have a snowmobile.'

'Still?' she echoed. There wasn't much point asking Alex. He knew that she wanted out, and he hadn't offered to help her. She swallowed and wondered what was going to happen now.

'...if you're still here tonight you sleep at my place.'

Of course nothing would happen even if she did spend the night on his sofa. But he must intend to try to...to seduce her. Why else would he...?

'...put in storage when Alex left,' Joyce was saying. 'But I don't think he sold it, so now Alex is back the snowmobile has to be somewhere.' Joyce squinted out of the window. 'With the snow coming down like that,

I imagine he wouldn't take the helicopter up, but the snowmobile...' Joyce shrugged.

Sarah pushed her hair back with a hand on either side. It promptly curled forward again around her face. 'Joyce, what do you mean, when Alex left?' She didn't want to ask about him. He'd called Vancouver to ask about her, and she'd told herself that it was a business tactic because he was on the other side of this negotiation over Aunt Lori. Except that he'd made that insane wager, and how in God's name could she have been crazy enough to agree to the terms?

'College,' Joyce said. 'He did high school in Smithers, like all of us, but then his parents sent him off to UBC, then after he graduated he got that scholarship to McGill and afterwards he was in that big brokerage in Toronto.'

'Big brokerage?' She could well be spending the night in his house, at his mercy. If there were weapons she could find, she'd better find them. 'What big brokerage house?'

Joyce said, 'He'd still be in Toronto, I guess, except that when his wife died he gave it all up.' Joyce had tears in her eyes just thinking of it. 'He just walked away from everything when she died. His whole life in Toronto, everything that—— He just left it all. He came back here and he built that house up on the hill as if he would never go back.'

Sarah got up abruptly. 'I—I'd better get back. Thanks for letting me use your phone.' She wished she hadn't asked about Alex. Joyce was watching her with curious eyes, and Sarah had an uneasy feeling that there would be gossip running around Elizabeth Lake. About the city stranger who wanted to know all about Alex Candon.

Joyce said, 'I saw you in his truck.'

'He's my aunt's landlord, remember?' She managed a smile. 'Sorry, but you're wrong if you think I'm interested in your mayor. I have a job that keeps me very much occupied. I'm too busy to start a romance with anyone.'

'That's sad,' Joyce remarked.

This whole thing was getting out of hand. A crazy bet. Aunt Lori putting signs outside her window. Joyce acting as if she felt sorry for Sarah when this was the nineties and a woman didn't have to be attached to a man to live a good life. Joyce, of all people, feeling sorry for her! Joyce, who spent her winter mornings shovelling snow, between washing nappies and feeding her dog!

Sarah said goodbye, but once outside she turned away from Aunt Lori's. She couldn't go back and face her aunt's irrational conviction that the universe was unfolding as it should. Instead she stuffed her hands inside her coat pockets and ploughed her way along the streets. She passed several people out with shovels, one older man who grinned and stuffed his shovel into a snowbank as she passed.

'I quit!' he announced. 'I'm going inside to watch the hockey game, and I'll come out when it's stopped falling.'

Sarah stopped to ask him, 'When do you think that will be?'

'Couple o' days,' he guessed.

'You don't know anyone who's got a snowmobile, do you? I need someone to give me a ride out to Smithers today. Actually, out to anywhere on the main highway.'

He shook his head. 'You don't want to go out in this. Can't see a darned thing; you'll run right up against a tree. 'Sides, it'll be dark soon. Gets dark early up here in winter—you're from down south, aren't you?'

'Yes,' she agreed. She thanked him and walked on, slipping once and almost falling on a piece of ice hidden under the snow. She walked slowly, watching her footing after that.

* * *

When she returned darkness had begun to flow over the town of Elizabeth Lake.

The lights from the houses reflected brightly off the snow as she walked back towards Aunt Lori's apartment. Sarah could see everything; white falling snow, white houses and the shadows of vehicle tracks through the snow. It looked like a dream scene, the lighted windows of cosy homes, glimpses of fire flickering in stone fireplaces, warmth to draw close to.

She found Alex's truck parked outside fourteen Cory Lane.

He had come to claim his winnings. He had won her for a night. It was ridiculous! Outrageous, and he could hardly hold her to it, except that she would have demanded he pay up if she'd won, and he would have honoured his promise. She took her bare hand out of her pocket to open the outside door. Her gaze dropped to her leather boots. He would tell her she was crazy, out walking his snowy streets in city boots.

She *was* crazy. Until today she had *always* played safe, avoided risks. That was one reason Stellers Gardens was still solvent. Other hotels had gone bankrupt, expanding over-optimistically with the good times, crashing with the recession. But Sarah had family, responsibilities, and she'd learned to be careful from a very cautious businessman—her father.

She opened the door and the warmth drew her in, but the uncomfortable image of her father was still with her as she climbed the stairs. He would turn in his grave if he could see her now. If she had any sense she would run, but there was nowhere to run. Just upstairs, and she climbed those stairs very slowly. She could hear their voices when she opened the door to Aunt Lori's apartment. They must be in the living-room. Had Aunt Lori offered to give him a cup of tea? Had she offered to read his leaves afterwards? Sarah hoped not. Alex hadn't much time for that kind of thing and Lori would be wise not to antagonise her landlord further.

Sarah took her boots off quietly. She couldn't hear much of what they were saying. She caught a couple of words. Something about herself, then the words 'plane crash' and that was Aunt Lori, telling Alex about the crash that had taken the lives of both her husband and Sarah's father.

Sarah didn't like her name associated in that account. She had been the one to take over once her father died. The natural choice, because he had trained her. Everyone knew that, but Sarah felt uneasy about the way Alex seemed to be collecting information about her, about her family. It made her feel vulnerable, as if he were a threat that would reach past the bounds of Elizabeth Lake.

She tiptoed into Aunt Lori's guest-bedroom and closed the door, but it emitted a loud squeak as it swung shut. Now they would both know that she was back. She should have gone to the living-room to say hello, but her tights were wet, as were her trousers. She changed into another pair of tights, another pair of wool trousers. She put on a blue sweater over them. The sweater was Aunt Lori's, offered earlier because Sarah hadn't packed for the climate up here. It was a bulky knit that was loose and almost shapeless, perfect for tonight.

Sarah wasn't about to wear a thin blouse, not with the prospect of Alex Candon's eyes travelling over her with leisurely possessiveness.

She swallowed and stared at herself in the mirror. Her hair was still down, unruly waves reaching past her shoulders. Normally she had it done every morning by the girl from the hair salon on the main floor, twisted back in a knot that was both businesslike and elegant.

She couldn't possibly manage to duplicate that style by herself, but she had to do something. She didn't want to go out to Alex with her hair curling everywhere in wild abandonment.

She grabbed a brush and the pins and struggled with it until it was anchored and contained. She reached up both hands to twist in a stray strand and the sweater pulled against her, forming soft wool to the curves of her breasts. She dropped her arms abruptly and fought the surge of trembling that swept over her.

She was *not* going to think that kind of thought! She squeezed her eyes tight and tried to gather calm strength around herself. It wasn't easy; calmness wasn't natural to her. She lived and worked on tension, on pressure and deadlines. Somehow she had to relax and persuade herself that the man out there wasn't a threat, had to believe that or he would see the truth in her eyes.

Of course he wasn't a threat. It was just awkward that she'd let herself get caught in such a ridiculous situation. He'd warned her, had told her that he usually won. Well, she had lost. She would pay her debt, but afterwards there would still be Aunt Lori's eviction to worry about.

She put on lipstick with a trembling hand, pressed her lips tightly together and stared at herself in the mirror until she decided that she looked reasonably normal. Then she took a deep breath and went out to the living-room.

Aunt Lori looked up from the sofa, her hands pressed tightly together. 'There you are, dear! If you hadn't come back I'd have sent Alex after you. Did you have a nice walk?'

'Yes, thanks.'

Alex looked comfortable in the big easy chair. He had watched her walk into the room the way a man watched a woman he was intimate with. Sarah felt the heat that had crawled up her neck and into her face.

'Hello, Sarah.' His voice was lazy, amused by her embarrassment.

'Hello, Alex.' She didn't meet his eyes. 'I did have a nice walk,' she said hurriedly, keeping her eyes on her aunt. 'I must have talked to ten snow-shovellers, and I stopped in a tea-shop, a really nice place.'

'Martha's,' said Alex.

'Of course.' She managed to smile at him, the cool smile that she used for hotel guests who thought they could make out with the manageress. 'You'd know it was Martha's, of course.'

'He was born here,' said Lori. 'And it's the only tea-shop. Now why don't you two enjoy a nice talk while I get the supper on the table?'

'I'll help,' offered Sarah.

'No, it's all ready. Just sit down.'

Alex rose up from his chair easily, smoothly, and gestured for her to sit down on the sofa. Would he sit beside her if she did? Uneasily, she sat right at the end.

'Nervous?' he asked softly.

'No,' she lied. 'Did you get the snow-plough fixed?'

'By morning, I'm assured.' He sat back down in the big chair. He had a glass of something in his hands. He lifted it and took a sip. Aunt Lori didn't tolerate spirits, so heaven knew what it was she'd given him. Sarah's lips twitched and Alex said, 'It's some kind of herbal thing. She may think it's a spell, but if you've roped her in to defeat me don't count on it working.'

'Aunt Lori doesn't do spells, just tea-leaves. Is it minty tasting?'

'Yes.'

She nodded. 'When I was a child I used to call it "the cure". I don't know what she puts in it, but it tastes great when you've got the flu.'

'I'll remember that.' He smiled and she didn't seem able to stop her lips curving in response.

She said, 'The charter people said they called the town and the runway wasn't ploughed.'

He put his glass down, half finished. 'If I'd told them to come ahead, they wouldn't have been able to land.'

'I know. But you have a helicopter, don't you? And helicopters don't need a runway.'

'You've been doing your research, haven't you?'

She shrugged. 'What else did I have to do today except try to get out of here?'

He stood up as she pressed back in her seat, but he moved to the window and stared out at the falling snow. 'I wouldn't fly anyone out of here in this weather unless it was an emergency. I'm sure you tried the helicopter charter firms, and they must have told you the same.'

'They said the visibility wasn't good enough.' She stared at the back of his head, the warmth of the dark waves that he must have brushed into submission.

He turned to face her. His mouth was straight, the lips full and frowning. She wondered what he was really thinking. 'I didn't sabotage your efforts to get away, but I wasn't about to help you, either.' His eyes swept slowly from her face down to the curves that Aunt Lori's sweater hadn't managed to conceal and he told her softly, 'I intended to win.'

She said stiffly, 'You haven't won anything but an awkward night.'

'We'll see, won't we? What are you going to tell your aunt about why you won't be back tonight?'

Sarah swallowed. 'Maybe the truth, but it's not your affair, is it?' Her face flamed. Affair. That was a bad choice of a word.

'How old were you when your father died?'

A muscle jerked in her jaw. 'Is this what you do? Collect information and use it against your opponents?' He said nothing and she snapped, 'I hear you used to be king of the sharks in Toronto.'

'How old?'

'Twenty-five. Why is it your business?'

'Were you close?'

She snapped back, 'Why did you leave Toronto?' and gasped because that was a terrible thing to ask when she knew the answer was rooted in the tragedy of losing the woman he'd loved.

'I wasn't satisfied with my life there.'

An evasion. He wasn't about to start confiding in her, telling her about his pain. She frowned and looked at her own hands clasped in her lap. 'My father—yes, we were close, mostly over the hotel. I started working there part-time while I was still at high school. I think he felt most comfortable there, at the hotel, and—well, we didn't talk about it, but we were close.'

'Supper!' called Lori. 'Come and get it!'

Alex reached a hand out and took hers. He pulled her up and she came to her feet very close to him, staring up and feeling his impact in her heartbeat. He lifted her hand and brushed the backs of her fingers across his cheek.

'You must miss him,' he said gently. 'I'm sorry you lost him.'

'It's been a long time now,' she replied quietly, although he was right. She wanted to tell him she was sorry about his wife's death, too, but she could not get the words out. The thought of Alex with a wife was disturbing.

Over dinner Lori looked brightly at Alex and said, 'I'm so glad you're here. You can help me with a problem.'

Sarah thought Alex suppressed a choking sound. They'd eaten and talked, but there had been no mention of Aunt Lori's illicit activities. Sarah knew that Alex was suppressing amusement, but it was anyone's guess what her aunt was thinking.

'Alex, I want you to take Sarah off somewhere. I don't want her here tonight.'

Sarah choked. 'Aunt Lori!'

'Well, Sarah, you know how I feel about this.'

'About what?' She could feel her face flushing. This was outrageous. Her damned aunt was playing match-maker! That's what the whole thing was about. She understood now. Lori had let this eviction thing get out of hand deliberately because she'd found an unattached man she thought Sarah should meet.

'Aunt Lori, just exactly——?'

Lori snapped, 'You always laugh about my tea-leaves, and I can't concentrate. And, much as I love you, I don't want you here while I'm having some friends over for tea.'

Sarah sagged back in her chair. Trust Lori not to have the sense to keep her mouth shut about tea-leaves in front of Alex!

Alex pushed his plate back. 'Why don't I take Sarah off, then?' Sarah glanced at him warily, but his face gave nothing away. 'Are you ready, Sarah?'

She wasn't. She never would be. This was danger and she had always avoided risks. But it was a tide sweeping her along, and she found herself dressed in coat and boots and leather mittens, walking out to the truck with Alex.

Silently.

She didn't know what to say.

She glanced at him warily, but he didn't show any emotion at all. Inside the truck she wrapped her arms around her knees and stared through the windscreen as he drove slowly through the snow in low gear.

'I don't know what you're going to do,' she said unsteadily. 'About Aunt Lori, I mean. She's—she's just Lori, and she's always been a bit scatty, but it's getting——' She spread her hands helplessly. 'I know you've got grounds to kick her out, and I—well, I can't talk her into behaving, or moving out or——'

She jerked her head away and stared out of the side-window. It was disconcerting, talking and watching his face and seeing no response at all. She gulped and said, 'You can see how she is, can't you? Nothing makes an impression unless she wants it to. And—well, it didn't even matter to her, saying she was having friends for tea even though you were there. If you'd asked her if she was going to read tea-leaves and let them pay, she'd have told you.'

'Yes,' he agreed, and it was amusement in his voice, not impatience.

Lori had done it deliberately, tossing Sarah out with Alex, hoping to stir romance. She had not meant to be cruel, but it was a terrible thing to do. Sarah shivered and said, 'It's like trying to hold back a waterfall with my bare hands. I can't get her to stop any of it!'

She would have to go back to Vancouver and leave the whole thing up in the air. That meant worrying about her aunt, feeling helpless and frustrated and waiting for disaster to come. She said unsteadily, 'Would you just call me if—well, I guess when—when you actually have to kick her out?'

'I won't kick her out.'

She jerked around and stared at the tightly drawn lines of his profile.

'Why? It doesn't make sense if—— Why not?'

He shrugged. 'Nothing's going to stop your going back, and that leaves her up here without anyone. She might be driving me nuts, and I'll keep trying to make her see sense, but I'm not pushing her out.'

Sarah winced. 'You make me sound—she's the one who chose to come up here, and I can't just move up here because she settled away from her family. I've got my work and responsibilities in Vancouver and——' She hugged her knees again.

A thickly bundled form stepped in front of a snowbank ahead of the truck. Alex slowed to let the sexless bundle cross the road.

Sarah asked, 'Would you actually have enforced the eviction if I hadn't come?'

'Probably not. It was a strategy which failed in its objective.'

'To make Aunt Lori see reason?'

'Yes.'

She glanced at him uneasily. 'You don't like me much, do you?' She'd thought he did, had felt a warmth with his eyes on her. He obviously found her physically attractive, but he didn't like Sarah Stellers, the person, very much. 'Do you?' she asked again, because he didn't answer although he glanced at her with one disconcerting flash of icy grey eyes.

He turned at the corner and pushed the truck into an even lower gear. The abandoned car was still on the hill, but now it was only a big mound of white snow, the car hidden under it. Sarah hugged her knees tighter. This was insane. Going home with a man who didn't like her, spending the night. Her penalty for losing, but she had been a fool to agree to those terms.

'Why do you want me at your place tonight?' She bit down on her lips after the words escaped. A night alone with a man she hardly knew!

'Call it an impulse. A gamble.'

'When you don't even like me?'

'Did I say that?'

She swallowed. He hadn't, but . . .

He turned into the drive and pulled out a little device that sent his garage door up. She asked tonelessly, 'You ploughed the snow away?'

He parked inside beside a low, gleaming car. 'I paid Kelly to do it. The high-school kids were grounded today since the highway isn't open for the school bus, and Kelly's been short of cash ever since he discovered girls.'

Sarah got out of the truck and moved to the car, letting her fingers trace along the dark blue hood. He was watching her. Always watching.

She said tonelessly, 'A BMW seems a suitable car for a stockbroker. You brought it with you when you left Toronto?'

He opened the door that must lead into the house. 'Coming?' he asked.

She followed him up the stairs. They emerged in the entrance foyer she remembered from yesterday and he turned to face her. When he began untying the belt of her coat she jerked back, but there was nowhere to go. She was backed against the wall of his foyer, staring at the melting snow on his waving hair.

'I—I can do that myself,' she protested.

He released the belt and reached to undo the coat's top button. Her breath caught in her throat. 'Why?' she whispered. 'Why am I here?'

Slowly he freed each button, then he put his hands on her shoulders and turned her. She moved mechanically, her arms co-operating as he slid the coat off her shoulders and down her arms. From behind her he said, 'You know why. Because I want you.'

Want.

'I——' She turned around and he was too close, holding her coat in one hand. He was studying her. Looking for cracks, she thought wildly. This was a man who was an expert on assessing his prey, whether it was an unpredictable stock or a woman he wanted. 'Do you think I'm just—just going to—to fall into your bed because you—because I lost a bet? Do you?'

'No, not because you lost. For other reasons.'

What she saw in his eyes made the heat crawl up her neck and into her cheeks. He saw the colour and reached to touch her flushed cheek.

She jerked her head away. 'Don't!'

'Do you think I'm going to force you?'

'No! I—back off and give me some room! Please!'

He stepped away from her and she bent down to unzip her boots. 'I suppose I think you're trying to—to seduce me. But I don't—well, to be blunt, I——'

'You what?'

She stood up, aware that she'd lost two inches of height shedding the boots, that he was too tall and too broad and entirely too much a very masculine man. 'I don't seduce that quickly.'

His lips twitched. 'Is that as blunt as you get?'

'No.' He was the one who was blunt. Asking for a night from her, telling her he wanted her when they hadn't even . . . when . . .

She whispered, 'Did you think I would . . . would——?'

His voice was muffled as he hung her coat up, then his own. 'No, Sarah, I didn't expect you to fall into my bed this quickly.'

She backed away towards the living-room as he turned away from the cupboard. 'Then what's the point?' she demanded warily.

He followed her. She had to keep moving because he would not stop. She ended up standing with her back against his bookcase and staring at him as he kept coming closer. He said slowly, clearly, 'The point, Sarah, is that I want you, but I'm not about to follow you back to Vancouver to get you.'

She crossed her arms in front of herself, aware that she was doing that a lot, that he made her feel defensive. 'Do you suppose if... if you followed me, that I'd—I'd comply?'

'Comply?' His eyes were laughing. 'Yes, Sarah. If I followed you, you'd become my lover. If I tried... yes, in time you would.'

She wished she could look away from him, wished she could control the things that happened to her body when he talked about possessing her as if he knew that she would have no choice in it. As if it were a magnet and she were made of iron filings.

'Why?' she whispered. 'Why wouldn't you follow me?' This was awful! She couldn't be asking that, as if she ached to have him following her back into the life she led, invading the walls in the place where she belonged.

He stepped closer and brought both hands to frame her face. She found her head tilting back as he pressed gently with his thumb under her chin. She felt her lips parting and forced them to press together.

'To be honest...' His fingers traced the shape of her lips. She hoped that he couldn't feel the trembling that grew up, her body fighting against her will. Lips wanting to soften and part while she forced them together into a hard line. 'The last thing I need in my life is a relationship with someone like you.'

'You mean—you brought me here tonight for a one-night stand?'

He shrugged. 'Let's say I thought it was worth a try.'

She jerked away from him and swung to face the rack of compact discs under his stereo. She pulled one out and turned the case over, trying to make out the name of the songs.

'You don't want a relationship with someone *like* me?' Her voice rose. 'What am I like?' She was *not* going to cry. It would be ridiculous to cry when a man said he didn't want a relationship—when she didn't want it either. She muttered, 'And what makes you think I would——? The last thing I'm after is a man in my life! I——'

'Sarah——'

'Don't!' She swung to glare at him. He was leaning against his bookcase and she wished there were some way to make him stop staring at her. She whispered, 'I'm not going to listen to you tell me what's wrong with me. And if you think that bringing me here is going to make me decide to—to——'

'Go to bed with me?'

'Yes,' she snapped. 'No! I mean, no! It's the last thing I'm going to—— Oh, hell!'

She paced across his room, back towards the foyer, unable to make any sound on the thick carpet. She stopped, glaring at him across the width of the living-room, and said grimly, 'I don't want to be seduced, so what alternative entertainment do you have planned for the evening?'

When he moved she jerked back.

'Relax, Sarah.' She watched him warily, but he moved to the console built into the wall. 'I think we can manage to amuse ourselves, don't you? Music? Perhaps a movie?' He gestured to the video-recorder built in below his television, opened a cabinet near the player and pulled out a rack of videos. 'Why don't you choose one?'

She still had the compact disc in her hand. She moved slowly back and put it in its place, then went to the rack of movie tapes.

'And you never know,' he drawled softly from behind her back. 'You might decide in the end that sharing my bed would be a good way to spend the night. I can promise you, we'd both enjoy it.'

CHAPTER SIX

SARAH stared at the television screen, concentrating on the actors and their words. She had followed the story with determination, although she was constantly aware of Alex near by on the sofa.

Sarah had chosen the easy chair, avoiding the sofa that would be comfortable for two people. She was concentrating on the movie, but every time Alex moved she felt her body stiffen. She told herself not to look, to ignore him, but she saw him pick up the remote-control. He pushed a button and the burly blond actor on screen froze in mid-word.

'How about some popcorn?'

'Yes.' She stood up thankfully, aware of the restlessness that had been with her all evening. 'If you show me where things are, I'll make it.'

'No problem.' He was on his feet, rejecting her offer of help with a smile. 'Put on some music. I'll make the popcorn.'

She frowned, watching him walk towards the kitchen. She wasn't the kind of woman he wanted a relationship with. He had gambled for the chance at one night, but she was not getting into his kitchen or his life—just his bed, if he could arrange that. And, if he couldn't, she thought that it did not matter very much to him.

She did not want the relationship either, so why was she so upset by his attitude? Why was she hurt at the way he carefully kept her outside certain invisible barriers, like the open archway leading to his kitchen?

She tried to find music that wasn't romantic, but the first song on the album she chose was about loving and losing. There wasn't any loving here, although she had certainly lost. Alex had warned her that he usually won his gambles. Luckily for her, the evening wasn't turning out to be all that painful, if she kept her mind off the fact that Alex Candon had reservations about Sarah Stellers, although he wanted her.

The film was fun. Sarah had found herself laughing more than once at Alex's criticisms of the photography and acting. He wasn't a man who let himself be buried in the story. He watched critically, and Sarah enjoyed his comments. The directing *was* rotten, although she personally liked the lead actor.

She had never thought of film-watching as a social thing, but with Alex it was. He was good company, if only she didn't find herself wondering what it would be like to feel his arms around her, his lips exploring her mouth with passion.

She could find out if she wanted.

She turned the music louder, trying to drown out the images. She had trembled when he undid her coat, but that was nothing to the thought of his hands releasing the buttons on her sweater...cupping her breasts through the lacy fabric of her bra... seducing the clothing away until she was naked, his lips coming down to possess her nipple...then...

She had to stop this! It was only cabin fever, her imagination going wild because she could not use her energies in work. She would fill her mind with concrete images. Nothing sensual. Physical things like...the sound of the popcorn exploding in the kitchen. Did he have a popper? Was he doing it in the microwave? Why hadn't he wanted her to make the popcorn?

He didn't want her in his kitchen. He didn't want her in his life. Just in his bed for a night. Maybe he had another woman. Not someone in Elizabeth Lake or Joyce would have said something. Somewhere else. Or perhaps——

Perhaps he didn't want anyone to take his wife's place in his heart. Three years, Joyce had said, but if he'd loved her deeply he might stay faithful in his heart for the rest of his life.

She sat down as he brought in one big bowl of popcorn.

He put the bowl down on the long coffee-table in front of the sofa, then crossed to the chair and caught her wrist with his hand. Her lips parted in protest as he pulled her to her feet.

He said quietly, 'Is there any reason you can't let yourself enjoy tonight, Sarah?'

She swallowed and tried to look away.

'Why not, Sarah?' His voice dropped and the husky tones made her tremble as he said seductively, 'Tomorrow you'll be back in your world. If not tomorrow, the next day. But meanwhile——'

She whispered, 'I'm not...'

'I'm not going to bite you, Sarah.' His lips widened slowly into a smile. 'I only brought one bowl, so surely we can share?'

She sat down beside him on the sofa, strongly aware of the length of his thigh beside hers. She shifted so that they weren't quite touching and he flashed her an amused glance that made her flush self-consciously. He lifted the bowl and put it in her lap. She knew that she was being silly, but she could feel his strength even though they weren't touching. She could smell the soap from the shower he must have had earlier, and the faint tang of his aftershave.

After he pushed the button to start the film he put his arm along the back of the sofa. Behind her back, not quite touching her shoulder. He was twisted slightly towards her, reaching into the bowl for a handful of popcorn every couple of minutes. She tried to lose herself in the film, but it had begun to drag.

'Someone should light a bomb under the leading lady,' said Alex wryly. 'This scene would be a lot more moving if she would stop posing and get some life into her.'

'She's every man's dream, isn't she?'

'Some men want a real woman, not plastic perfection.' His hands moved from the back of the sofa to touch the knot of her hair.

Sarah felt her scalp shudder. She stared at the screen, at the perfect sex symbol there, her body twisted into a pose that someone must have thought alluring.

Alex murmured, 'A man likes something to undo, something to uncover. A little mystery.'

She could feel his breath on her neck, the movement of warm air shifting strands of hair that had escaped. 'What are you doing?' she demanded in a strangled whisper.

'Taking the pins out.'

'I... Why?' She hugged the bowl of popcorn tightly and stared at the screen. She could tell him to stop. Each light touch of his fingers in her hair sent sensation crawling along her scalp and down her neck, all along her spine.

'I want to see it, touch it.' She could feel the mass of her hair beginning to fall as he told her in a voice that made her shudder, 'You have beautiful hair. Lovely. This morning, when I saw you... all free and curling, lush and wanton.' His fingers found the last pin and she felt her hair falling, his hand tangled in it, encouraging it to be wild.

She turned, the bowl still held tightly in her arms. His gaze came slowly from her hair, tracing the curve of her jaw, her cheek. His fingers caressed the hair, moving it, making her hair touch the places his gaze touched. Softly.

She felt the heat surging through her veins as his eyes stopped at her lips. He was going to kiss her. He took the bowl away and she did nothing to stop him. On the screen the lead actress was dancing with the hero, moving her hips suggestively.

Sarah whispered, 'I'm not...' as Alex's lips moved closer. She felt her own mouth moving, her lips parting, her tongue touching the sudden dryness. 'Don't,' she whispered, but she ached for just the touch of his lips.

His thumb found her lips and explored. When it slipped between her lips she saw something change in his eyes. She realised then that she had bitten down on his thumb in a sensuous caress. Wanton, he had said, talking about her hair, but his voice had said it was the woman he meant, too.

'I'd disappoint you,' she whispered.

'I'd take a bet on that,' he said huskily.

'You don't—you can't *always* win your bets!' She had to stop stammering, but her insides were shaking, her mind spinning with images from the movement of his hands on her hair and her face.

'I'm not losing this one,' he promised as his lips came to hers.

She backed away, pressing into his hand at the back of her neck, feeling his fingers moving on her nape and her scalp through the erotic silk of her own hair. She gasped and tried to think of something to say, because if he kissed her——

'You—you said you had family here. Who——?' Her voice was squeaky. 'What kind of family?'

His lips had been parted to take hers. Now he smiled slightly and with one finger he stroked her lips, her chin, the tender flesh under her jaw. 'My father's the town doctor,' he said softly, possessing her chin with his hand, raising her mouth and brushing his over her lips, then retreating.

She licked her lips. 'Your—your mother?'

His mouth took possession of her lower lip and tugged gently, then released. She heard a faint moan from her throat as he murmured, 'She's an artist. She does landscapes in oils, teaches art at night school in Smithers.'

'Do you——?'

His mouth found the softness below her jaw. 'My brother Garth is personnel manager at a nearby pulp mill.' He moved his thumb along the place his lips had touched, then filtered his fingers through her hair to trace the shape of her ear. Then, when she was spinning from nothing more than sensation, he bent over her and kissed her eyes.

'He's...married?' She couldn't see anything. Her eyes were closed, her senses concentrated on the softness of his lips on her eyelid, on her cheek, her mouth.

'To Edie,' he said softly, his hands on her shoulders, fingers curving into her softness to possess her as he brought her closer. 'She's visiting her mother in Arizona right now. They have one boy. I told you about Kelly. And Edie—she's allergic to dogs.' His lips brushed her mouth again, then retreated.

Sarah knew that she should run, but his hands were on her shoulders and there were other parts of her body crying for touching. As for her lips, she could feel them swollen although he'd hardly touched them. Swollen with aching need.

'I have a sister, too,' he continued slowly, his gaze clinging to her mouth. 'She's a paediatrician in

Vancouver, married to a history professor at UBC.' Suddenly he was very still. 'You're driving me mad, Sarah. You've had that effect on me from that first moment out at the runway. Is there anything else you want to know before I kiss you?'

She drew her lower lip between her teeth. 'Where's— where's your dog?'

'I told Kelly to take him home for the night.' She swallowed. Alex said, 'He's used to having the run of the place.'

On the screen the voluptuous actress shouted that she would not give herself to a man who wanted only her body. Alex's hands slid down across her back, his fingers spread out so that she felt each one through Aunt Lori's sweater. He bent his head, blocking out the world as her eyes flew open.

Then he kissed her.

Kevin had kissed her often and intimately in his campaign to persuade her that she should give herself to him before the wedding. She was a cold woman, he had told her in the end. Other men had told her that she was cold, and she had believed it because no one stirred heat and passion in her blood.

Alex kissed her slowly, moving against her with leisurely softness. He teased her lips, bringing a flush to her mouth, to the flesh everywhere, as if the blood was surging faster to heat her flesh. Her hands were in her lap and she lifted them, telling herself that the movement was a protest.

Her hand found his chest. He was wearing a soft brown and golden sweater and she felt her fingertips probing into the wool, pressing into the hard curve at his breast.

He moved away and her mouth followed. Then he brought her closer, trapped her hands between them, her

own breasts crushed against the backs of her hands.
'Close your eyes,' he commanded.

Darkness possessed her, then his mouth. Her pulse
grew heavy. When her breathing changed he touched her
lips with his tongue, stroked the sensitive flesh and found
his way inside, taking her deeper into the kiss.

His hands were stroking, exploring the curve of her
spine, the rigid muscles on either side. She made a throaty
sound without knowing it was hers. He took her mouth
more deeply and her body, deep inside, began to throb
with a rhythm which she could not hold back.

His hands slid into her hair and he held her head as
he probed the secrets of her mouth, teasing her tongue
and her lips, making them greedy and restless until she
was driven to discover the secrets of *his* mouth, giving
and taking and shuddering deep inside.

She whimpered when he pulled away.

Her hands were curled into the softness of his sweater,
digging into hardness below. Her eyes were wide and
vulnerable and she could see her own needs reflected in
the grey of his eyes staring down at her. She touched her
lips with the tip of her tongue and felt them swollen and
wanton. She moved her head to feel his hands on her
scalp, felt the wildness of her free-flowing hair
everywhere.

'Sarah? Do you want to run away?' His voice was
harsh as his hot gaze swept over her trembling body.

'I——' she swallowed '—I don't know.'

From the television someone shouted, 'I'll get you,
you bastard!'

Alex slid his hands away and she sank into the sofa.
She felt his fingers combing through her hair, twisting
to let the curls cling. Then he drew her hair forward and
she felt it curl down over her shoulders. He traced the
path of a curl as it twisted down. She stopped breathing

when his finger crept lightly over the sweater, down towards the slope of her breast. When he altered course, circling the swelling of her breast, not touching the hardening peak, she heard the sound and it was her voice, whimpering.

'You're coiled up like a spring,' he whispered. He moved his hand back along the path it had taken, back into her hair. Her body clenched in reaction to the places he touched, or perhaps to the places he did not touch, because she could feel the caress he had not made as if it were fire in her breasts, flames licking down the centre of her, making her hot and tight and helpless to fight her own weakness.

He took her shoulders and curled his fingers around them. 'It's been a long time, hasn't it, Sarah?'

Oh, God! She stared back up him, his eyes probing through everything, so deep.

'If you're going to run away from this...' He slid his hands across her chest, pressed against the swelling of her breasts, cupping her in his palms, making her want to cry out, to move and touch and feel. Then, abruptly, he was motionless. 'You'd better run now if you're going to.' His voice turned harsh. 'If you don't, Sarah, I'm going to get under that skin of tension you're wearing.'

She made a sound. Not a word, just confusion and need and helplessness tangled together in a noise from her throat. His hands took the weight of her breasts through the sweater. She felt the air going out of her lungs in a long sigh.

'Sarah?' She saw him swallow and he closed his eyes tightly. 'Sarah, you've never done this before, have you?'

'I—no.' Her lips were dry. Aching.

He pulled his hands away. Her own hands fell into her lap. On the television there was shouting...insults and crashing of furniture...a free-for-all fight.

He said huskily, 'It never occurred to me that you were...'

She felt her fingers curling together. 'A virgin?' Suddenly the heat from the fire burning in the hearth seemed to flow over her, flushing her face and turning her blood to burning. She whispered, 'Would you have cancelled the bet if you had known?'

She saw his throat spasm. He said abruptly, 'Get your things on. Your coat, and... I'll take you back.'

He would be in her dreams. She would be haunted, aching. All he had done was kiss her and touch her breasts through her clothing. He hadn't even begun to seduce her, but she would be dreaming that forever.

She said hoarsely, 'Aunt Lori doesn't want me there. Not tonight.'

'I'll take you to my parents.' A muscle jumped in his jaw. 'You can stay there.' She didn't move and he said harshly, 'Now, Sarah! Get your coat.'

She touched his face and he jerked back. 'Damn it, Sarah! I don't want——'

'Earlier——' Her voice was husky, uneven. 'Earlier you said you did want me.'

Aunt Lori might be ninety per cent crazy, but she had brought Sarah here for Alex Candon, and for once perhaps Aunt Lori was right. Sarah was afraid that if she walked away from this man now she would regret it for the rest of her life. She put her hands on his chest, palms pressing against his hard muscles, fingers spread out to explore the shape of him. She felt the hard collision of his heart against his chest, heard the explosion of air sucked into his chest.

'Damn you,' he whispered as his mouth came down on hers. There was nothing slow or soft about his kiss. He took her mouth with his deeply, harshly, sweeping her further and faster than she was ready to go, then breaking away and leaving her breathless and bruised somewhere deep inside.

'Get your coat,' he growled.

He stood up abruptly and moved to the window, pulled the heavy drapes aside and stared out. She felt alone, empty, staring at him with eyes so wide that she couldn't even blink. Sarah didn't know where it would lead or what would happen to her life if she reached out and let this man possess her. She'd felt his tension, his need when he kissed her. If she went to him now...

She had told him that she was not a girl for taking risks, but she knew that it was too late to turn back from this danger.

She said quietly, 'You named the terms, Alex.'

He did not turn to look at her, but she could see the tension in every line of his body. He laughed harshly. 'The last thing I want is a workaholic virgin dedicated to the city. Damn you, Sarah! This wouldn't do either one of us any good!' He turned and glared across the room at her.

She'd been gulping for air, shaken and ready to reach for him, to pull him close and forever. She whispered, 'You said you wanted to make love to me. If you want me, I'm here.' She was offering herself to him. She wouldn't have believed she could do that, that any man could stir her enough to make her say words like that. But it wasn't just his lips touching, his hands possessing. It was his eyes, and the knowledge deep inside her that this was meant to be.

'No,' he denied harshly. 'Not with you.'

She closed her eyes painfully because he was telling her that the loving all belonged to his wife who had died. She stood up and someone on the television shouted that Ellie was pregnant and, damn you, what are you going to do about it?

He was lying. He had to be lying. She could see it in his eyes. She picked up the remote-control and the voices went silent, the screen blank. She dropped the control and stood erect and made herself move towards him, one silent step after another on the thick carpet, her fingers curled in on themselves so that her nails dug into her palms. She saw that muscle jerk in his jaw when she stopped in front of him.

'One night,' he ground out. 'That's all. I thought you were an experienced woman, that you knew exactly what——'

'I'm a woman,' Sarah said, and she felt fear. He had promised her that he would not be disappointed, but she *was* completely inexperienced and he'd expected more than that.

Alex said, 'I'll protect you,' as if the words were driven from him, then harshly, 'Damn you, Sarah! Don't do this!'

She uncurled one hand to reach out to his arm. She could feel muscles there, hard, rigid. He growled, 'After tonight I'll never see you again.' His voice was hard, but she could see his eyes. He added flatly, 'I might call you about your crazy aunt, but that's all, and I'd probably write if I had to, not call.'

She moved her hand to his chest. His breathing was shallow, more disturbed than his voice revealed. He might think they could be together tonight and forget it after, but he was going to find that he was wrong. She knew that there would be more. She could feel it, somewhere inside. If there was a power called love between a man and a woman, then it was growing now, the pull between them, and he was caught in the trap as surely as she was.

She placed her other hand on his chest and he told her in a low voice, 'We're going to regret this. We're both going to regret this.' He must be trying to make his voice cold, but she could hear the lie.

She said softly, 'No, Alex, we aren't.' She moved her hands up, curling her fingers around his shoulders. She threaded her fingers into the waving crispness of the hair at the back of his neck, watching him, her gaze moving, sweeping over his face as he stared down at her.

It was ice in his eyes now and she bit her lip, drawing her hands back from him and feeling the flush flowing over her skin, knowing that he was watching her and she was throwing herself at him, and he really didn't want it at all. She swallowed, standing so close, not touching him now, knowing that she hadn't the courage if he was going to look at her like that.

'Do you want me to go?' she whispered.

She stepped back and she was glad that he'd said he would never see her again, because it *was* indifference in his eyes and she'd been wrong to believe that he was burning inside and the fire was more than both of them. Recognition, as if they were two parts of one entity.

She backed up another step, but he came after her, slowly, his eyebrows so low that she could see only shadows where his eyes should be. She stopped and he was there and his hands cradled her face and she closed her eyes and felt the shudder through her whole body.

Slowly he drew his hands away from her face, drew a line of tension down her arms and circled her wrists with his fingers. He drew her hands up, slid them on to his shoulders, then he brought her close with his hands hard against her back, exerting pressure to bring her body against his, bending to take her mouth in a slow possession that made her eyelids droop down heavily and her breath come in ragged jerks.

'Alex...'

He left her then, left her standing alone. She didn't watch him, but she heard the sounds. One light went out. Then another. The music started, but it was different now, slow and seductive. When he came back he was going to take her into the bedroom. She could feel the nervousness swelling up with every step he took in the journey towards her.

'Dance with me, Sarah.'

He drew her close. Her arms were around his neck, hands splayed out on the backs of his shoulders, feeling the roughness of the wool of his sweater, wandering into the swirl of hair at the back of his neck. His hands rested on her hips, bringing her close as she moved to the music.

It was unlike any dancing she had done before. Slow music, notes pulsing along the synapses of her nerves. He turned and her leg slipped between his. A low sound escaped his throat and his hands slid up, learning the shape of her through the bulky sweater. She turned her face and buried her head against his shoulder, but he took her chin and lifted it up so that his mouth could search out the softness of her lips.

She lost herself in the kiss. His mouth, his tongue, invading, possessing. Her hands, restless, needful, finding the tangle of his hair at the back of his neck. Trying to bring him closer. Her body moving with the rhythm his touch taught.

A moan. Hers, the sound against his open mouth. His hands, seeking warmth under the bulky sweater she wore.

When he found the contained curves of her breasts under her sweater she whispered his name on a sigh. His thumbs sought the peak of her nipples through the fabric of her bra, driving strength from her, making her cling and close her eyes tightly as the world went spinning. He found the front clasp of her bra and then his hands were warm and intimate on her breasts.

She whimpered and he took her mouth more deeply, and he must have known that she could not stand on her own any more because he swept her up into his arms and then she was going down, sinking, lying on the carpet with his head a silhouette coming down over her, and his hands on her under the sweater, stroking and caressing and turning her voice to formless cries of need and pleasure.

Sarah tried to find her way through the barrier of his clothing, to touch him, her hands seeking restlessly. Alex pulled away from her and stripped his sweater off, came back to place her hands on the hard place where his heartbeat throbbed.

Slowly he began to undo the buttons of her sweater.

'One,' he whispered, and his mouth found the warm flesh exposed while his hands sought under the wool, stroking and caressing.

'Two.' His fingers parted the wool, his mouth seeking the beginning of her woman's swelling. 'Three...oh, Sarah...so lovely...'

She moaned...could feel his heated breath on her before his lips took possession. He kissed her breasts, touched fire with his tongue, teased her nipples to aching, seductive madness that left her writhing in his arms as he seduced her with words of love and desire that left her clinging to him and gasping.

When his hand slid down along the curve of her hips she was moaning from the caress of his lips and his tongue, and her breasts were naked now, flushed and heavy and aching with need. He was driving her wild, teasing her with kisses on the warm slopes of her breast, only occasionally taking the peak into his mouth, knowing that she was aching, heat pulsing heavier with each caress and pulse gone wild with the teasing wandering of his lips along the warm curves.

'I knew you'd be like this,' his husky voice whispered against her throat. He took her hair and spread it everywhere. His lips sought her through the wanton waves of her lush hair. Then he possessed her breasts with both hands, the curls of her own hair lying on the warm slopes, and he tortured her with his mouth, moving from one swollen peak to another.

When she cried out his name he stroked her thighs slowly through the woollen fabric of her trousers, so that his name was only a whisper and a moan.

'So lovely,' he whispered, and her hands clenched in the tangle of hairs on his chest as he slid the last of her clothing away from her. 'So warm and soft and wanton.' He touched her then, finding the moist heat of her centre so that she whimpered and somehow managed words.

'Alex—please! I—can't... please... please love me now.'

He took her then, with his hands and his mouth and his masculine body. She felt need and pulsing and deep, aching throbbing growing wilder and wilder into breathless agony and passion... spiralling into whispers and moans and ragged anticipation torn from his lungs and hers, racing for the breathless explosion, crying out with arms tangled around each other, bodies closer than close, buried, losing the world in spinning dizziness that left her exhausted and clinging in his arms.

There was only silence and darkness when she woke.

An arm around her hips, holding her against warmth. Slow, deep breathing on her shoulder. She opened her eyes and it was shadows on shadows. She closed her eyes again and he was everywhere, holding her, possessing her with his body all along her back while he slept, his arm thrown over her hip to bring her close against him.

They were in a bed, covered with a deeply lush quilt that held winter away. Alex stirred and Sarah could feel the quilt shifting on them both. His hand slid up to possess her midriff and he murmured something low and formless in her ear.

What in God's name had she done? She trembled and he was still sleeping because she could hear his breathing now, lower and slower and sounding as if he was breathing through his open mouth, bathing her shoulder with warmth and stirring something insane inside. If she turned in his arms, touched his chest and moved against him...

He would wake and she could feel from his sleeping body that he would wake reaching for her, touching and caressing and drawing her back down into the madness. She swallowed and felt the flush of memory crawling over her. His low voice murmuring words that blended with his hand and his mouth on her, his body possessing hers, and somewhere in the raging wildness her voice, and it couldn't be true that she'd lost control that badly but she had screamed his name in the dark and he'd answered with his body.

She had to get out of here!

She jerked away from the arm holding her and she heard him murmur something that might have been her own name. She was standing now, beside the bed, shivering because the heat must be turned down for the night and the warm shelter of that quilt. She stared and she could make out the lump that was his body under the covers. He was a big man and if she had thought to be afraid last night she might have feared giving herself to him. But he had been gentle, had driven her ahead of his need so that even the sudden, sharp pain in the moment of possession had been buried in the throbbing in her veins, the aching pulse beating through her woman's body. If he woke now——

She hugged herself, feeling her own nakedness.

He had warned her.

'After tonight I'll never see you again. I might call you about your crazy aunt, but that's all, and I'd probably write if I had to, not call.'

On the bed Alex made a sound that might have been a low groan, then turned on to his back, his arm thrown out and his breathing settling into slow, deep sleep.

She found her clothes in the living-room. There was a faint light from the foyer, flowing in to make form out of the shadows. She dressed, shivering as she untangled her tights from her trousers, found her bra and that bulky sweater of Aunt Lori's that she hoped she would never see again. She did up every button and she could feel just what she had felt when he had slowly, agonisingly freed one after the other.

Her boots. Her jacket. At least it was downhill going back, and surely Aunt Lori's evening tea party would be over by now! If not, Sarah would burst in on them and they might think she was a ghost because she was so pale. She belted her coat tightly and she couldn't find her bag, but then she remembered that she hadn't brought it. She hadn't brought any of the things you would bring if you were staying the night.

The clock on the video-recorder said it was three. Late, but not morning yet. That made her a welsher because the penalty for losing her wager had been a night with him and the night wasn't over.

She went down the stairs to the garage and out past his truck and the BMW. Outside the air bit into her lungs when she breathed, but there were stars everywhere and the world was almost as bright as daytime, each bit of skylight reflecting on the world of white.

The snow was crunchy under her feet. She kept stepping on to it, then breaking through. This was what she needed—brisk night air to drive sense back into her mind. She had spent twenty-nine years being sane and rational, making the decisions that made sense. She'd been the kind of child who was told over and over again how grown-up she was. And now——

Twenty-nine years, but the rebellion and insanity inside must have been saving up, collecting into a big ball of madness, just waiting to explode. She got to the road and it was downhill then. Her boots were insanity in this kind of terrain, the heels throwing her off balance as she got to the slope of the hill. Trying to go down, slipping because there was ice under the snow.

She tried to wriggle her toes inside her boots, but the only thing was to hurry, to get to Aunt Lori's where there was warmth and shelter. Halfway down the hill and she would be at the bottom soon. She put her foot down and it must have been pure ice in that spot because she felt herself sliding. She gasped and tried to recover, throwing her hand out towards the white mass of the abandoned car, but it was too far away.

She heard her own voice crying out, and a sound like a crack as she fell.

At first there was no pain. Just shock, her lungs tearing, trying to get air in. The first breath that came was tearing and loud. Then Sarah felt the nausea turning to growing agony. That crack, and she'd heard that sound years ago, on a ski-hill. Only this time there were no skis, and no ski patrol. This was a little town, asleep. How long would it be until someone came?

Hours, perhaps.

Maybe her ankle wasn't broken. It must be possible to have that kind of throbbing pain without an actual break. Just because she'd once broken her leg...well, it could be a sprain and the cold probably made it worse. She felt the pain in her hand, but that was ice and trying to hold herself still. She jerked her hand away and her ankle screamed.

She huddled, hunched over, trying not to move and fighting a wave of dizziness. She'd better not faint. She was in the middle of the street. Somehow she had to pull herself off to the side. A truck could come, run her down, because she was hidden between mounds of crunchy snow.

She stared at the thrust of her legs, concealed by her coat. She thought she could feel the ankle swelling, wondered if there was blood and didn't want to look because what could she do?

She closed her eyes and the pain was worse, far worse than the time she skied off the trail. On the ski-slopes they had sent out search parties within an hour, and it might have seemed forever, but she had known from the beginning that they would come to find her. Here, in Elizabeth Lake, no one would come.

Alex.

She closed her eyes and willed him to come, but he had told her that he would never want to see her again. When he woke alone he would probably be relieved to find her gone.

She couldn't believe she'd thrown herself at him after listening to his harsh voice telling her that it would be nothing, that he cared nothing for her, only desire for one night and possession and then nothing at all, forever.

Oh, God! Her ankle!

Mind over matter. She had to think about the pain as a small thing, fading away. She closed her eyes and maybe it was working, because she felt herself fading away. It must be shock, she decided dully. Her back clamped into a painful protest at the awkward position she was trying to maintain, sprawled on the road, trying to balance, unable to move her leg. She gasped and a spasm went through her with the pain from her back, then the jerking motion of protesting muscles reached her leg and everything went blank.

CHAPTER SEVEN

SARAH could hear Alex's voice, could feel his hands running over her, sensation muffled.

She moaned, 'Don't touch—don't—my ankle!'

She felt him moving her coat, bending over her and looking at her leg. Alex. He had come.

She opened her eyes and it was him, then she realised that she was crying and she gasped with pain before he could touch. 'Don't—can you see if it's broken? There isn't a bone sticking out or——?'

'No. Now stop worrying. I'll look after you.'

She closed her eyes and he was gone, then back almost at once. He smoothed her hair away from her face gently and she whispered, 'When I was fifteen I broke my leg. I was skiing, and—I—it seemed . . . so long . . . before anyone came. I didn't think you would come.'

'I'm here, Sarah. I'll be right here with you until the pain's over. Do you hurt anywhere else? Just the ankle?'

'Just?' She tried to smile. 'It's broken. I know it is.'

He squeezed her shoulder reassuringly. 'I'm going to slip your arm around my neck. I'll hold you, help you stand up, and we'll get to the truck.' Alex touched her face, brushing the falling snow away with gentle fingers as he asked quietly, 'Ready?'

'I——' She dragged in a shaken breath. 'OK.'

He moved carefully, his arm around her waist, hers around his neck as he helped her hop towards the truck. He let her set the pace, not touching her leg at all.

'Do you do a lot of this?' she gasped.

'A bit.' His face was harsh and lined in the light from the sky, but his voice was humorous as he said, 'I do have my industrial-first-aid certificate, if that reassures you.'

'An "A"-grade, I suppose?' She gasped at a twinge from her ankle.

'Of course,' he agreed. 'Just a few more feet, Sarah.'

Elizabeth Lake's jack-of-all-trades, she thought wildly, trying to ignore the agony as he helped her into the back of the truck. The mayor, the landlord, something to do with the minor hockey league. And now—— She suppressed a gasp, turned her face into his shoulder and bit hard on her lip.

'It's OK,' he promised her. 'It won't be long. Just a few minutes more. Hold on, honey.'

He covered her with a thick sleeping-bag. She cradled her foot and ankle gingerly with her arm. 'Where did the sleeping-bag come from?'

'I keep it in the truck.' She must have whimpered, because Alex said, 'Hold on, honey. Just a couple of minutes.'

'I'm OK.'

'You will be,' he assured her, touching her cheek before he moved into the front seat. She thought that it would hurt when the truck started, but he was an incredibly smooth driver. It couldn't have been far because a moment later he stopped and got out of the truck. She heard a door slam, then Alex's voice calling out, muffled by distance. Then the back of the truck opened and there were more voices, then arms, and she managed this time to bite her lip on the moan that surged up her throat. Voices around her, arms helping her inside. A deep male voice that she thought was Alex's until she heard him saying, 'Careful!' Then a woman's voice and Sarah kept

her eyes closed because if anyone wanted her to smile
or speak she simply couldn't do it.

'Not a pleasant welcome to Elizabeth Lake, is it?'
asked a gruff voice.

She opened her eyes. Bushy grey eyebrows over narrowed grey eyes. Harsh planes to a thin face with broad
cheekbones. Grey hair that must have been the same
warm brown as Alex's once, and shoulders that would
be at home on a football field.

She whispered, 'Dr Candon, I presume?'

He smiled Alex's smile. 'Right the first time. Now,
Sarah, we're going to take your coat off, then something
for the pain before I look at that ankle.'

'Close your eyes,' said Alex. 'Let us look after this.'

'It was the boots,' she whispered. Someone touched
her and she knew it was Alex. He untied the belt on her
coat, then released the buttons. She opened her eyes and
his head was bent so that she could just catch a glimpse
of the concentration on his face.

He murmured softly, 'This isn't a seduction. Not this
time.' She moved her hand in protest. His fingers caught
hers and she gripped tightly, hanging on as she felt the
needle going in. Then dizziness drifted over her. The
voices blended into confusion as Alex lowered her on to
something firm and cool.

Voices. The ringing of a telephone. Someone said
something about cutting the boot off, too much
swelling...X-rays. The roar of a truck outside. Alex's
voice telling her it was all right, honey.

'The helicopter...half an hour to clear the hangar
doors.' That was Alex's voice, talking to someone else.
'Kelly, get your gear on and give me a hand getting the
plough-blade on the Jimmy.'

Sarah opened her eyes when a middle-aged woman bent over her. She was grey-haired with frowning lips below warm eyes. Alex's mother?

Someone was lifting her. Not Alex. She knew his hands.

'Where's Alex?' she whispered.

A hand came down on her shoulder. The doctor. Alex's father. Strange, how she was learning to know people by their touch. Very strange, because there wasn't much touching in her life.

'He's gone to get the helicopter ready. You'll be tucked into the Smithers hospital before you know it.'

'Don't like...hospitals.'

Someone laughed and Alex's father said something about a broken ankle being a good thing to take to hospital. Then the strange man was joined by another and she must be on a stretcher because the bed underneath seemed to come up with her. The lights overhead moved, making her dizzy.

Managing Stellers Gardens with a cast on her ankle was exhausting. Sarah's ankle ached whenever it wasn't elevated.

Her busy days felt oddly empty, the nights far worse. Night after night she woke and reached for warmth and found nothing but cool sheets on the other side of the bed. She got out of bed when that happened, pushing the emptiness away, forcing herself to concentrate on details that were immediate and demanding.

Anything to push back the memories...Alex's voice reassuring her during that night flight to Smithers...Alex holding her hand during the short ambulance trip...Alex gone, and a woman in white saying with a shrug, 'Mr Candon? He's flown home—just waited until the X-rays came down on you.'

Images of her own insanity, of passion and need.

Deliberately Sarah buried herself in the demanding details of her life.

She arranged to have Aunt Lori's telephone bills sent to the hotel, called her aunt every Sunday on the telephone. Lori was cheerful and vague. She didn't mention Alex Candon and Sarah did not ask. Sarah wanted to scream at Lori because this was all Lori's fault and Sarah believed that it had been a deliberate matchmaking effort. In a cruel way the matchmaking had worked. Sarah had reached and come away aching for things that she hadn't even known she wanted.

You couldn't call that winning.

Each Monday Sarah had dinner with her mother in the big old house where she had grown up. The weekly dinners were a habit that mother and daughter had followed for years.

'Sarah, you must come home to the Cassidy ball,' her mother insisted one Monday in early February.

Sarah shifted on the uncomfortable antique chair. 'A formal gown and a ton of plaster on my ankle?' She lifted another mouthful of food from her plate. Her mother had a new cook who seemed addicted to tasteless elegance.

'You'll be expected. And, incidentally, I need a new dress for that ball. If you could ask that accountant...?' Jane shrugged gracefully. 'You know what costs are these days.'

'I'll have some money transferred into your account.' This was her job, the task her father had left her. Look after her mother, her aunt, and her brother—keep the family business in the black.

At least Mike didn't cause problems. Her brother spent his dividend cheques on university fees and books and computers, and if he could think of another degree to go after once he had his doctorate in chemistry she didn't suppose it mattered much.

The next day was a nightmare. While Sarah was in a meeting with her accountant Bookings rang through to announce that the computer had snarled. They had twenty rooms double-booked and no cancellations. Sarah wondered if her father's ghost would haunt her if she just limped out of the door of her office with her cast, rode the lift down to street level and walked out. What would happen if she left them all to deal with the chaos without her?

Stellers Gardens survived the booking crisis and Sarah bought herself a new gown for the Cassidy ball. It was a long amber creation that drifted mysteriously as she walked. Looking at herself in the mirror, Sarah could imagine Alex's eyes watching her.

She had to stop doing that!

Her doctor took her cast off the day before the ball. After six weeks in plaster she felt rocky in high heels, so she sent out for low-heeled sandals to match the gown.

Louise came up from downstairs to do Sarah's hair with her cart and her buoyant cheerfulness.

'Just the usual,' said Sarah, knowing that it was going to be a long night. She never slept deeply or easily, but these last weeks had seemed even worse.

'The usual? With that dress?' Louise shook her head. 'A gorgeous dress deserves something——' Louise spread her hands expressively, then started taking the pins out of Sarah's hair.

With her hair down Sarah looked softer, more vulnerable. She didn't like that look on her face in the mirror. It was all too easy to remember Alex whispering seductive caresses.

*   *   *

Alex stepped out of range of Wanda Cassidy's clinging grip as someone pushed ahead of him to catch the socialite's attention.

Wanda's little party would be on the community news tomorrow, the success of the season. For Alex's taste there were too many elegantly dressed people, too much noise. He was damned if he was coming back to this nutty world, turning himself into a machine again, building new regrets, new pain for the future. The last three years had been good. He hadn't felt emptiness until Sarah flew into his life.

Sarah... Wild, clinging hair and soft eyes. She had been haunting him for six weeks and he knew that he should never have touched her.

Sarah Stellers and Alexander Candon could never be anything but disaster. He had understood that from the beginning. And now he couldn't sleep in his own damned bed without her scent and her hair and the breathless gasp in her throat haunting him!

At first he had told himself that the memory would fade. He had buried himself in coaching and the town council and the dispute with the government over the proposed flooding of the area to the north. The only trouble was, that was daytime stuff and the nights were the worst. So he started linking into the computer network earlier in the mornings, spending more time with computer and telephone and fax until he could feel the whole rat race crawling over him again.

Sarah's fault, damn her!

Then Lorraine Rooney turned up in his office wearing the sweater Sarah had worn that night. She presented him with her rent cheque and the letter that Sarah had said she would refuse to sign. She had plopped it down on his desk and announced, 'It says I won't take money from anyone, but I'm not stopping my tea parties.'

After the door closed behind Sarah's aunt Alex had thrown his damned coffee-cup across the room, smashing it to bits against the door that the crazy woman had closed as she went out. Not because of her, but because of that crazy sweater and the memories.

Sarah Stellers was damned near always on his mind.

Sarah... The breathless sensation of his hands in her hair... his mouth teasing tension from her mouth... her stiffness melting into passion.

His heart smashed against his ribcage in a violent response to that image. The reality of Sarah had been a hell of a lot more shattering than his expectations. She'd moved into his arms and touched him with hesitant hands on his chest, had admitted that she'd never been with a man before. And he'd felt so damned... well, he'd tried to escape, because how the hell could he keep up the fiction that it was just sex, that she didn't matter, when she was in his arms, so sweet and warm and giving him the gift she'd trusted no one else with?

Six weeks of hell, thought Alex grimly, glaring at the dance-floor that was seething with Vancouver's upper class showing off their expensive clothes. This need for Sarah was an addiction that he could not seem to fight. After she was gone he had growled at everyone in his family. He'd made Mary Anne's life hell for losing the minutes from the last council meeting. He'd even sold a block of stock that he knew damned well he should keep. In the twenty-four hours after he unloaded his Engar holdings he had received calls from five quiet, powerful men. Calls from Toronto and New York and London, from men who asked Alex what he knew that they didn't, and was Engar Corporation on the way down?

Then he had shouted at little Tommy Harridon for missing a goal he should have made, and Tommy had broken down into tears. It was shouting at Tommy that made Alex realise he had to see Sarah again.

Ambition and pressure, that was her life. Alex knew about ambition, but losing Denise had taught him that some things had too high a price. Sarah Stellers had too high a price, but he had only to close his eyes to remember the way she'd driven him wild with her own heat and passion. The first time for her, and he'd felt her soft tendrils wrapping around his soul because it was more than her body that she'd given him that night.

'Did you know Alexander Candon was here?'

'What?' Sarah jerked around to face the man who had spoken, smoothing the filmy fabric of her long, amber dress uneasily with her hands. She was in a circle of men—two other hotel owners, Jerry and Nick, and the investment broker who had made the announcement.

Jerry turned to the broker. 'In Vancouver? What do you think it means?'

'Actually, I mean *here*. At the ball.' The broker was scratching his cheek thoughtfully. 'Could be he's thinking of opening a branch here.' He grimaced and added, 'For the sake of my business, I hope not.'

Sarah dragged in a slow breath. She twisted and half expected to find Alex right behind her. He wasn't there and she felt a sick wave of disappointment settling on her stomach.

Jerry was saying, 'Retired from the financial scene, didn't he?'

The broker snapped, 'Candon left Toronto, but don't fool yourself—he's still in control of the brokerage firm.'

Jerry shook his head thoughtfully and Nick demanded, 'Who exactly is he?'

Sarah saw motion to her left. She turned in time to see Charles Kantos place a lean hand on Jerry's shoulder.

Charles towered over Jerry by a good eight inches and Sarah stared at him, remembering Alex telling her that he'd called Charles to find out about her. Charles nodded and she tried to smile back because they'd known each other for years in a casual way.

Jerry was saying something about rumours and Nick asked again, 'Yes, but just who is Candon?'

Charles said patiently to Nick, 'Are you asking for a capsule history of Alexander Candon?' He smiled at Sarah and started ticking off items on the fingers of one hand. 'Wonder-boy of UBC's commerce department. Masters and doctorate at McGill, revolutionalised stock-valuaton techniques with his doctoral thesis.' Charles was folding in a finger for each achievement. 'Refused an appointment at McGill and went into Dadlock Investments, saved them from financial ruin and attracted the big boys.'

'Dadlock?' Nick echoed. 'Big take-over?'

'Right,' agreed Charles, smiling lazily. Sarah had the uneasy feeling that he was watching her. As if he knew... Surely Alex wouldn't have told Charles about that night?

The broker said, 'But Candon didn't go along with Dadlock. They wanted him, of course, but he started his own outfit.'

Charles grinned, amused by the broker's obvious envy of Alex.

'The man's got the luck of the devil,' the broker grumbled.

Charles turned away from the speculation about Alex. His cool blue eyes swept down to Sarah's clenched hands. 'I hear you came back from the north with a broken ankle.'

'It's better now, thanks.' She was relieved that her voice sounded normal. She forced her hands to unclench. Behind her the broker was predicting that the bear market would turn next month and now was the time to buy back in. Nick murmured something about pointing out this Candon fellow because he wanted to talk to him.

'You won't get anything out of him,' growled the broker. 'But you could try asking him what he knows that made him decide to sell short on Engar Corporation last week.'

Charles asked, 'Sarah, did you have a pleasant trip north? Aside from the ankle, that is.'

'Business,' Sarah said, but his eyes were speculative as she swept the crowd behind him with her gaze.

If Alex really was here she could not face him. She would come apart. She turned desperately back to Charles and had the uneasy feeling that he saw too damned much. She snapped, 'I hear that you're in a new business. Providing information.'

Charles's eyebrows went up. 'Oh?'

'You told Alexander Candon all about me.'

'All?'

She bit her lip. 'You and he are friends?'

'Yes,' Charles agreed. 'Friends. He once saved me from bankruptcy, so the least I could do was to tell him the little I know about Sarah Stellers.'

She felt her fingers clenching and something in Charles's eyes told her that she wasn't succeeding in looking cool and unconcerned. 'I never heard you were in financial trouble.' She wondered when it had been, and why he had chosen to tell her.

'No,' he agreed. 'I really should add discretion to Alex's virtues.'

'Is . . . is he really here tonight?'

'I understand he intends to be,' Charles said idly.

She bit her lip. 'Do you know . . . why?'

Charles's eyes slid past her and settled on something behind her shoulder. He breathed, 'Ah,' and she felt her heart crash into her ribcage.

She shuddered in the instant before the hand pressed against the small of her back. The lightest touch, fingers pressing against her, a voice saying her name. She gulped and Charles's brows went down over his eyes thoughtfully.

She turned to face Alex. People had been bumping against her constantly, the room too crowded to prevent continual collisions. But she had known the instant Alex touched her. She told herself it was because they'd all been speculating, talking about him, bringing him to her mind.

'Alex,' she whispered.

If there was something to read in his eyes, she knew she could not find it. Grey eyes turned to slate, opaque and hard as they watched her trap her lower lip between her teeth. Dressed formally, he was somehow different, as if more of the man was hidden inside. Dangerously hidden.

'Alex,' echoed Charles. 'I see you made it.'

Alex murmured, 'Charles,' but his eyes were on Sarah. 'How's your ankle?' he asked quietly.

'It's—it's fine.' She cleared her throat and felt his gaze sweeping down over the unsteady rising and falling of her breast, then down to her sandals.

'Dance with me, Sarah.' His eyes flicked to Charles and he said with a slight smile, 'That is, if you haven't promised this dance to Charles?'

Charles murmured, 'Regretfully, no.'

From Sarah, Alex didn't expect an answer at all—just compliance. His hand pressed at her back and she couldn't seem to do anything but move the way he was urging her.

She said unsteadily, 'Charles never dances with anyone,' as if it were a protest, but Alex's arms were drawing her into the pack of people who were trying to dance to music drowned out by voices on voices.

He possessed her shoulders with his hand and turned her to face him. She felt his arm at her waist, his other hand trapping hers in a firm grip. The last time they danced had been in his living-room. Soft music, his arms holding her closely, intimately. This time he held her at a distance, guiding her movements while his eyes followed every curve of her hip, her leg, her body, until her motions became slow and heavy with the pulse beating through her veins.

Silence between them, crushing noise all around. She whispered, 'I can't hear the music.'

He brought her closer until the silky fabric of her dress brushed his thighs whenever they turned. Then the music stopped and a distorted voice began an announcement through a microphone. Sarah couldn't see, but Alex turned his head and looked towards the sound over the heads of the crowd.

'. . . want to announce that——' The amplified voice broke up.

Alex's lips moved.

'What?' she asked, but it was her own heart beating. She had told herself that it was the music, that throbbing pulse, but it was inside her. She had to get away from him. Just his hand at her waist and she was afraid that she might go anywhere he led without asking where he was taking her.

He began to move, his shoulders making a path through the pressing crowd. The amplified voice was saying something that Sarah couldn't follow. The only thing she could feel was Alex's hand on her waist. When he stopped she turned and there were people all around.

They'd escaped the throbbing noise back on the dance-floor, but the crowd was everywhere.

'Alex, I—thanks for the dance.' He was supposed to say that, not her, but she cleared her throat nervously and added, 'I—it's nice to see you again.'

'Is it?'

She shook her head helplessly. Not nice. Shattering. 'Why are you here?' she whispered.

He looked behind her, his gaze sweeping the crowd. Someone said, 'Hey! Candon!' and his hand tightened on her waist. He said, 'Come with me. Let's get out of here.'

She felt her breath go out in jerks.

'Come with me.'

Once Kevin had said those words. She had told herself that it was her responsibilities that had held her back. Impossible, she'd told Kevin. She needed time, under-standing, couldn't leave when everything was in chaos.

If it had been Alex asking, she felt a panic-stricken conviction that she would have said yes. It wasn't love. Love wasn't destructive, pulling a woman towards madness and loneliness and losing everything just to put her hand in the grip of a man who had said that he wanted only her body for one night and he would never see her again.

Why was he here?

Their progress was stopped by the incoming crowd at the door. Alex muttered something about Wanda Cassidy not understanding the meaning of the words 'a select few' and Sarah choked on a hysterical laugh.

'Justin,' she said, remembering abruptly. 'I can't—I came with Justin Rule.'

'You're leaving with me.'

She stared up at him, her heartbeat suspended. He still possessed her waist with one arm, but he was facing her now and he was close enough that she could feel his heat and something else radiating from him.

Tension.

She breathed, 'Alex...'

Suddenly, Wanda Cassidy was there, touching Alex's shoulder with one hand and screaming over the din, 'Alex, darling! I consider it a special victory!' She gripped Alex with long, thin fingers. 'You haven't been *anywhere* in ages, and that you should choose my little party for your return to society——'

Alex interrupted, 'Do me a favour, would you, Wanda? Find Justin Rule and tell him I've taken Sarah Stellers home.'

'Darling Alex! You simply can't leave yet!' Wanda's free hand fell heavily on to Sarah's shoulder. 'Sarah, it's that bloody ankle of yours, isn't it? You do have bad luck! I remember that skiing mess you got into. You were in plaster all spring.'

Alex said firmly, 'Thanks, Wanda, and it's an incredible party you've thrown here!'

'Incredible?' breathed Sarah when they emerged into the damp night air. She saw his lips twitch in the beginning of a smile.

'Incredibly awful,' he muttered. 'What in God's name possessed you to go to the damned thing?'

'It's one of those things you have to do.'

There was a fine rain falling. Alex pulled Sarah back against him as she started to step out from the sheltering overhang at the stairs. 'Why was Wanda around when you broke your leg on the ski-slopes?'

'I went to school with her daughter.' If he could be nosy, so could she. She asked, 'Why did you sell off Engar Corporation?'

'A moment of damned insanity. Don't you have a coat? Do you go through life this way, shivering?'

'It's in the cloakroom.' She glanced back at the crowded doorway to the hotel. 'It'll still be here tomorrow, or Justin might get it—he's got the claim-ticket.'

Alex murmured something to the doorman and a limousine appeared from nowhere. The white-gloved driver held the door while Alex stepped back and ges-tured Sarah inside. She climbed in and sank into the deeply lush seats.

Where was he taking her?

CHAPTER EIGHT

SARAH could hear Alex's voice giving the limousine driver an address near Sunset Beach, an area filled with high-rise condominiums and apartments clustered close to the financial district. She turned away when he climbed in, worrying her upper lip with her teeth as the limousine moved slowly into the rainy Saturday-night traffic.

He sat beside her. Staring through the window, she was aware of the quiet hum of the partition behind the driver going up, sealing her in with Alex. She knew that she should ask where he was taking her. She felt motion and turned to see him push one hand through his hair, sending the smoothly disciplined waves into unruly curls. She felt nervous, and panic and hope tangled together, but he appeared to be completely calm. Her gaze followed the path of his hand and her fingers remembered the sensations of caressing his hair.

'Alex, I——' She jerked her head away, desperately staring out of the window. She had to do better than this! How could a man's presence paralyse her will, leaving her aching and wishing for things that she didn't know how to reach for?

He said coldly, 'I'm not about to attack you, Sarah.'

She traced the bottom of the window with her index finger, concentrating on the way the faint layer of condensation from the rain outside fell on her skin. She said, 'I wanted to thank your family for helping when I broke my ankle. Your father was great.' That was better, her voice steadier. 'And your mother. I remember her, but I never got to say—and Kelly, wasn't it? Your nephew?

127

I was groggy after your father gave me that injection, but I heard you asking Kelly to do something with the plough.'

She glanced at him, caught a brief flash that might be impatience. He said, 'Kelly rigged the blade on my truck and ploughed the hangar doors clear so I could get the chopper out.'

'And you,' she went on tonelessly. 'Thank you for—for coming and finding me. I'd have gone mad out there, alone until someone came at daybreak.'

He replied harshly, 'You would have died of exposure. Were you so desperate to get away from me that you had to risk your life?'

She studied the street outside, the bus passing the limousine. She tried to blink the tears away. 'I—I'm not very good at awkward situations.' She closed her eyes painfully and one damned tear escaped, making it impossible for her to turn and face him. She whispered, 'The morning after wasn't part of the wager, was it?'

'Look at me, Sarah.'

She shook her head, leaning forward, wishing that she could concentrate convincingly on the dismal rain outside. 'The snow is prettier,' she commented in a brittle voice. 'Your winter is prettier than mine. And thank you. For coming when I was hurt.'

'I did get your thank-you note. And my parents got theirs.'

She tried to keep her face averted, but he was touching her, one hand in her hair and the other cupping her chin and urging her to face him. She gasped, 'I—I forgot to send my medical-plan number to your father.' She bit her lip. 'He never sent me a bill either. I—I'll give it to you, shall I?'

'If you want.' He brought her face around and she closed her eyes because she couldn't stand to see impatience or criticism in his eyes.

'I don't have my bag with me. It's back at the hotel. I could——'

'Send him the number. Mail it. Relax, for God's sake! What do you think I'm going to do to you?'

Sarah bit her lip and felt the dampness on her lashes as she opened her eyes. 'I'm—I'm not very good at——'

'Awkward situations?' Alex's thumb brushed the dampness from her cheek. 'That must be inconvenient for a hotel manager.'

She licked her lips, fighting the urge to close her eyes again, to give herself up to the rhythmic stroking of his thumb on her cheek, her jaw, the soft flesh that stretched towards her throat. 'It's not—in the hotel I know what my role is supposed to be.'

She wished his heavy brows did not shadow his eyes, although she thought she wouldn't be able to read them in any case. He asked quietly, 'Is that what bothers you right now? That you don't know what your role is with me?'

She thought the lump in her throat would strangle her. 'I—yes.' She drew in a shaky breath. 'You told me you never wanted to see me again after——' The limousine stopped. Another red light, she thought vaguely. 'So why——?'

Alex's fingers tensed on her chin. 'We've arrived.'

'Where?'

'My apartment.'

'I didn't know you had an apartment in Vancouver.'

She knew nothing about him. He had let her think that he was a small-town mayor, that he lived a lazy life of bits and pieces. Once he had warned her that he won his gambles, but she hadn't understood the extent of what he was saying. He was a man who never had to accept losing. It was frightening, remembering the way he'd say he'd wanted her, wanted a night with her, and she had walked into his house as if his wanting was all it took to enslave her.

She clenched her hands together to try to stop the trembling. 'Why?' she asked shakily. 'Why are we going up to your apartment?'

'We can be alone there.' The door was opening and he said harshly, 'We don't have the kind of conversations that should be public.'

She stared at the open door, the driver waiting silently. Alex's territory. He'd always had that advantage with her, keeping her off balance. She whispered, 'We could go to the hotel. I have a suite——'

'And a telephone that rings?'

The door was wide open now and Alex had his hand on her elbow, urging her out. She whispered raggedly, 'I can't go up there with you without knowing what—what you intend for—for...us.'

His voice was harsh, low, and his fingers bit into her elbow. 'I imagine that it will be a disaster, but we're going to be lovers.'

She felt her throat clench and he was putting pressure on her arm, and the driver was out there, holding the door. 'How long?' she whispered, then closed her eyes because she couldn't believe she'd asked it that way, with her heart aching in her voice. She moved, passing from Alex's hand to the white-gloved courtesy of the limousine driver as he helped her out on to the pavement.

'Until it burns out.'

There was another doorman at the building, murmuring Alex's name and ushering them through a silent glass door. Then a lift with a courteous, uniformed operator who recognised Alex with a respectful nod.

'Until it burns out.' The words echoed endlessly.

They stood side by side behind the silent lift-operator. Going up to the penthouse. Sarah stared at the numbers as they rose in silence. When the doors opened silently she moved out on to the carpeted corridor. She thought she would scream when his hand came back to her waist, guiding her. Silently.

They were going to have an affair. Until it burned out.

He opened the door to the penthouse with a security card.

Sarah walked past him, along the corridor that was lushly carpeted and ridiculously wide for a space that had no real function except as a passageway. She was moving like a plastic doll, one foot after the other. Her ankle started to throb as she moved towards the thread of light in his sprawling, elegant living-room.

One wall was all windows and she walked towards it, driven by some desperate need not to be closed in with the man beside her. She found the latch of a sliding patio door with her trembling hand and slid it open, then walked slowly out on to the covered balcony.

He had a view of everything up here: the line of lights along English Bay, the bright towers of the financial district. She shivered in the cool night air, then turned and faced him, her back to the lighted skyscrapers, her hands spread out along the rail behind her.

'You're filthy rich.' Her voice was flat, accusing. 'This penthouse, and you call limousines, not taxis, and when you make a move the market erupts in wild rumours.'

'What rumours?'

She lifted her hands in an impatient gesture. 'You sell a stock and you tell me it was madness, but everyone believes it's a prediction of the future.'

'Then they're fools.' She saw the planes of his face as shadows on shadows.

'Charles says you saved him from bankruptcy.'

He waved his hand dismissively. 'What does any of that have to do with us?'

'I can't have an affair with a man I don't know.' Sarah shook her head and felt the curls brushing along her bare shoulders. 'I don't know who you are! I thought—but—but you're a shark, not a—and——' Her voice dropped to a whisper. 'I'm afraid you'll—I'm afraid...'

Alex's voice was quiet, very soft. 'You don't have any choice, Sarah. Now come inside, out of the cold.'

If he had taken her in his arms she thought she would cry out because she was too tightly wound, too driven with tension to do anything softly or quietly or easily. But he didn't touch her. He stepped back and she was past him, inside, the door to the patio sliding because he was closing them in together. She moved across the broad expanse of carpet towards the wall that had music and television and rows of books between.

'How long?' she asked, staring at the titles on the shelf, feeling his presence in the room behind her. There was no light reading here. Financial stuff. Some titles she recognised, some she didn't even understand. She swung around and he was over there at the bar, pouring something into two glasses. 'How long, Alex? How long do you give this...this...affair until it burns out?' She caught her breath as he straightened up with the two glasses in his hands. 'What are you doing?' she breathed. 'Do you think I'll be more...more co-operative after a drink?'

He was coming towards her. She hugged herself tightly with her arms clasped under her breasts. He held the glass out to her and she took it, her fingers clenched tightly around the fine crystal. She stared at the liquid and it trembled, too.

'Alex, I don't know how to have a casual affair. I just can't...handle it.'

He took the glass away from her and set it somewhere. Her gaze followed it, then he put his own drink down a couple of inches away from hers. He had just given the drink to her. She looked up and stared at him with her eyes so wide that she couldn't seem to focus on anything else.

With his hands on her wrists he unfolded her arms from their clutch on her body. He lifted one of her hands to his face and pressed his lips to the inside of her wrist. She tried not to feel anything, but the shock of his mouth on her flesh came out as a gasp, painful and breathless.

'It if were casual, Sarah, it wouldn't be a problem for either of us.'

The air went out of her lungs, leaving her dizzy. It was terrifying, what this man did to her. He took her shoulders in his hands and she felt her body sagging with surrender. Then he lowered his lips and took her mouth in a kiss that tore a whimper from somewhere low in her throat.

When she was nothing but mindless need in his arms he pulled away and said harshly, 'I'm not going to make love to you, Sarah. Not tonight.'

Alex stayed in Vancouver for four days. For Sarah it was four days of tension and uncertainty.

The tension was with her always. 'Lovers,' he had said, and her memory of one shattering night in his arms in Elizabeth Lake haunted her dreams and her imagination. 'Until it burns out,' he had said, but she knew it was a life sentence. The fire would be with her forever.

It was ironic that she should succumb to the spell of a man who wanted only enough of her life to destroy her.

Years ago she had believed Kevin when he told her that she was the ice lady. Kevin had loved her, and Sarah had believed she loved him, too. She enjoyed being with him and she felt warmth when his lips took hers, but his kisses never stirred her to impatience with the endless delays in their planned wedding.

After Sarah's father died Kevin had demanded she come with him, leave her work and her family behind. It had hurt, hearing his ultimatum, knowing he was telling her that he didn't see how impossibly she was trapped by the hotel. She had understood then that there was really no room in her life for loving. No time.

Until Alex drove into her life, his headlights coming out of the snow. From the beginning something in him had reached out to turn her habitual tension to restless fire. She had spent less than three days in tiny Elizabeth Lake. Three days that had melted Vancouver's ice princess into a river of need that might drive her insane. Then six weeks alone in the middle of hotel chaos, haunted by a few hours that would never leave her.

She had known her fate the moment she heard his name in the chaos of the Cassidy ball. If he asked she would have no choice but to give him everything. But Alex didn't want *everything*. He was very definite about exactly how much he wanted.

'I'll pick you up at eleven tomorrow morning,' he told her as he dropped her off at her hotel, hours after leaving the ball. 'I'll take you for a long lunch. You'll be back at the hotel by two.'

She had a meeting with her accountant at ten-thirty tomorrow. She would have to cut it short because something in Alex's eyes wasn't going to accept any changes to his schedule. She would have to be the one to change appointments, to fit her demanding life into the hours when he did not want her.

'All right,' she agreed tonelessly, standing beside the limousine, knowing that her own doorman was behind her somewhere, watching and wondering.

'And tomorrow evening,' he added. 'I'll pick you up at six.'

'I have to know when I'll be back.' She stared at his tie. 'The hotel—things happen.'

'Tomorrow's Sunday. Don't you take days off? Don't you have an assistant?'

She bit her lip. 'Yes, but——'

'You need someone competent to manage as your assistant.'

'Are you trying to tell me how to run my own business?' Perhaps it would be easier if she could feel anger, but even that protest seemed weak and resigned.

He said grimly, 'You're not running that hotel, it's running you.'

She remembered all the questions he had asked her, sitting in his darkened penthouse. She had thought that he wanted to know what was in her life, and she'd talked freely, even forgetting for a while the tension that had raged in her blood from his hands and his lips.

He could easily have taken her. All he had to do was reach, but he had destroyed her with a kiss and then moved to the wall, where he put on some music. He'd given her back her drink and led her to a deep easy chair, had sat on the sofa across from her so that he could watch her in the shadows while they talked in the near-darkness without touching.

She'd hoped that it was caring that made him ask questions. She had been wrong. He'd been assessing, judging, the way he assessed a stock he was thinking of buying. Or a stock he was thinking of dumping back on to the market, she thought miserably.

Outside her own hotel, between his limousine driver and her doorman, she said quietly, 'The hotel runs my life.'

'It's not going to run mine.' He touched her cheek and she jerked her head back. 'You should find someone who can look after all but the most important details. A manager. Why should it be you? You need more freedom.' His finger stroked down the tension of her cheek. 'If you're going to have a lover you need time for the affair.'

She whispered, 'Are those your terms?'

Something flashed in his eyes, but his voice was toneless. 'Tomorrow night you'll be back by two.'

Two in the morning. Were they going to make love? God knew why he hadn't taken her into his bed tonight, but he would reach for her when he was ready. He was the one calling the tune, not her. She thought of it that night, restless, wishing that quiet conversation in his apartment had been what she'd tried to believe it was. Wishing he cared, that he wanted the woman inside. Wishing it was more for him than that raging sensual thirst that had exploded back in Elizabeth Lake, or that she could at least have the strength to pull back from the affair that he said would end in disaster.

In the morning she told her accountant, 'I'm sorry, but we'll have to wrap this up in twenty minutes.' When he frowned she said, 'I can see you again this afternoon. At two.'

She blinked away tears as she hurried down to the front door where Alex had said he would pick her up. She supposed she should ask Alex for a schedule. A schedule—and that made it sound like something cold to be fitted in between her life and his, touching neither.

She couldn't run a business like this, telling her accountant that she hadn't time for him and hanging from one day to the next on Alex's whim.

The limousine was waiting. A different driver this morning, but he helped her in and Alex was inside, waiting.

'You look very nice,' he commented coolly.

She was dressed in a wool skirt and matching soft sweater with a scarf pinned around her throat. Her hair was up, fastened securely by Louise. If Alex took the pins out she would die of embarrassment when she went back to the hotel, walking in with a flush on her face and her hair wild and caressed.

He hardly touched her at all.

He talked as they drove to Stanley Park, telling her about the chaos down on Robson Street where some native rights demonstrators were holding up traffic. When the car stopped at the Pavilion he took her arm and guided her inside, where he ordered a salad for her.

She tried to eat it, but the first mouthful made her feel like choking. Crisp, fresh vegetables and she'd told him last night that she always ate salad for lunch, but she couldn't eat this one.

'Tell me about your family,' he commanded.

She wondered where families came when you were valuing stock, or if they only counted with lovers. How many lovers had there been since his wife died? Had he asked these questions of all his women?

'My family?' she echoed tonelessly. 'Well, there's my aunt.'

'Yes, I know your aunt.' It was the first time he had smiled at her that day and she felt some of the frozen tension around her heart softening.

'How is Aunt Lori? I talk to her on the phone, but she's vague about details.' He picked up his water glass

and turned it around and around with long, strong
fingers. 'She seems in fine form. She invited one of the
teenagers' mothers over for tea and now there's a constant stream of people coming and going from Cory
Lane.'

'She's not charging them?' Sarah worried uneasily.

He chuckled. 'She gave me a letter saying she wouldn't,
and I've stopped getting irate phone calls. I'm damned
if I'm going to start asking questions and stirring up
trouble.'

'You're afraid of my aunt?' Sarah didn't know how
laughter could come to her throat when she felt like this.

'Let's say I'm wary of her.' He grinned. 'Fighting
Lorraine Rooney could be more trouble than it's worth.'

She made her smile stay in place. Fighting Aunt Lori
had brought Sarah to Elizabeth Lake, and last night Alex
had told her that they were going to have an affair, but
he hadn't been happy about it. Maybe he didn't want
it, because he had kissed her and then pushed her away,
and now he was sitting across a table from her, making
no move to touch, asking, 'Are the rest of your family
cut from the same cloth as Aunt Lori?'

'Goodness, no!' She made herself smile. She had to
keep herself together somehow. It was easier with her
hair up. With the pins in place she felt more in control.
From now on she would keep her hair up. She tucked a
loose strand behind her ear and said brightly, 'My
mother's firmly involved in social causes. That charity
ball last night—she was on the committee. She lives in
the house I grew up in, on Marine Drive. She's—she
enjoys it.'

He put the glass down. 'You have a brother, too?'

She set her fork down and asked tightly, 'Why don't
you just ask Charles Kantos for the details?' He said
nothing and she sighed. 'My brother Mike is twenty-

four. He just got his masters in chemistry. He's at Dalhousie doing his doctorate.' She grimaced. 'He's doing his thesis on irradiating water to trace immeasurable bits of silicone and some other substance— I think it was silicone. His conversation gets pretty thick sometimes.'

'You're fond of him?'

'He's five years younger. I used to baby-sit him.' She stared at her salad and admitted, 'I used to think he'd take a degree in hotel management and that he'd end up at the hotel, too.'

If he had, she could have been free by now.

After lunch they walked slowly across the grassy park while he told her that the snow was still thick on the ground in Elizabeth Lake. In Vancouver it was a day that might almost have been spring. She thought that he would take her hand, but he didn't. They walked a couple of feet apart, talking about odds and ends and nothing much.

That evening he took her up the Grouse Mountain aerial tramway to look at the stars and the city. Not into his arms, and, despite the ache inside, she was slowly relaxing to his restraint. If it was only sex he wanted there was no reason for this delay. This was slower, and deliberate, as if he was courting her.

On the top of the mountain, looking down on the lights, she found the courage to ask, 'You were married, weren't you?'

'Yes.' It frightened her that there was no expression at all in his voice.

She stuffed her hands into her coat pockets. 'What...what happened?'

'She died three years ago.'

She knew that from Joyce, but she wanted to ask why and how and what part of his heart was back in the past.

The tone of his voice forbade questions like that, but she ached to hear him tell her that he felt more for her than flames that would rage and burn and die.

'Are you—are you thinking at all of marrying me?'

The top of the mountain was silent. The whole world was breathless, the sky and the lights spread out like a carpet below them. Alex turned and he didn't touch her.

'No, Sarah. Marrying you is the last thing I would choose to do.'

She had known the answer, hadn't she? It was some previously unsuspected urge to self-destruction that had forced the question out of her throat. He didn't even want to be her lover, had been drawn here by that uncomfortable passion between them. The last thing he wanted was her chains tying him forever.

But she'd asked anyway, as if she had to destroy what was between them before it could even start, blow whatever strange relationship they were going to have into shattered pieces because that was her only defence. She could not walk away, could not stop herself letting him see her aching loneliness. It was suicide and it would destroy her, but there didn't seem to be anything she could do about it. God help her, but she was in love with Alex Candon.

Jane Stellers said uncomfortably, 'Sarah, I think you're absolutely crazy.'

Sarah dropped her fork on to her plate. She had been toying with the cardboard casserole in front of her, repressing the urge to suggest that her mother fire her new cook despite the fact that he came highly recommended by Wanda Cassidy.

Her mother picked up her wine glass and stared at the dark red liquid. 'Last month you walked out of Wanda's party with Alexander Candon.'

Sarah tried to laugh. 'Are you saying that's evidence of insanity?' She tucked a strand of escaping hair behind her ear.

'You've been seeing him since then.'

'That's right. I'm seeing Alexander Candon.' Sarah managed to shrug. 'It's all over the gossip columns, so it's no secret.'

'Stop fooling with your hair, Sarah! You look a mess! You're not yourself at all these days. Where were you last Monday?'

'I called to tell you I couldn't come.'

'Yes, but where were you?'

Sarah pushed her plate away. Her mother was obviously upset. Sarah couldn't imagine why, but she knew that she would not handle one of her mother's concerned lectures tonight, although she couldn't understand the point of this one. She said in a brittle voice, 'I'll be thirty years old next month. Don't you think that's a bit late for this inquisition?'

Her mother snapped, 'Don't be crude.'

Sarah felt an urge to shout back at her mother, but the habit of their relationship was too deeply ingrained. A Stellers did not shout or brawl or do anything crude. She aligned her fork and knife neatly on her plate, then tucked her napkin under the edge. 'I was with Alex. Do you want details? Do you want me to tell you that we're lovers?' She stared at her hands, wondering bleakly why she had said that and knowing the answer.

Because they weren't. Alex had been back every week since the Cassidy ball. Sarah had lunched with him every day he was in town, had gone out with him every night. They had been to a dozen restaurants, to three movies and one concert. They had spent one afternoon sailing alone on Charles Kantos's boat. They had been paired together on the society page of the newspaper several times, and she knew that the whole of Vancouver assumed they were lovers. But Alex had not kissed her once since that first night in his penthouse apartment.

Their relationship made no sense at all. He wasn't her lover and although sometimes it felt like courting he had been brutally honest in telling her that he had no intention of marriage.

'Of course you're lovers,' her mother said with weary resignation. 'I'm not naïve, for heaven's sake, but what do you imagine you're going to get out of a relationship with that man? If you want money, Sarah, I suppose he might part with some, but you don't need it, do you? We're not skirting the edge of bankruptcy?'

'No,' Sarah replied. 'Of course not.' She thought uncomfortably that bankruptcy would be a relief, would free her of the hotel. She pushed her chair back. 'Is there some point to this? Some reason you want to warn me off Alex?'

Her mother sagged in her straight-backed chair. 'Sarah, don't be a fool. It's useless trying to compete.'

'Compete?' Her fingers clenched in on themselves. She whispered, 'Another woman? Alex and another woman? I—I don't believe it.'

'Do you think I can't see that you're making a fool of yourself over him? What do you think you'll get out of it? Sarah, I don't want to see you hurt. If you expect he'll marry you——'

Sarah stood up abruptly. 'Nobody's talking marriage, mother. And—I'm sorry, but I can't talk about this.'

She was halfway through the door from the dining-room when her mother's voice caught up with her. 'Sarah, you can't compete with a dead woman. Did you ever meet Denise Candon? The woman was gorgeous, and brilliant. How the hell can you fight a ghost?'

Sarah felt sick all the way back to the hotel in the taxi. She supposed her mother was right. Alex's wife was the reason why he could not love her back. He had loved his wife. Everyone seemed to know that he'd left his Toronto life in grief and he'd never gone back. If she needed proof it was easy enough to find. When she had asked Alex about his wife he had not told her anything, as if the grief was still locked inside.

If he didn't want to love her, why couldn't he leave her alone?

There was a message waiting for her at the hotel. Alex's name, and his telephone number up in Elizabeth Lake. Sarah phoned him from her suite.

'Hi,' she said breathlessly when she heard his voice. 'It's Sarah.'

'Hi, yourself.' He sounded like the Alex she remembered from the trip north. Quietly amused, and she could feel warmth in his voice. 'What's up in Vancouver?'

She leaned back on her sofa and closed her eyes, hugging the receiver close. 'Wanda is planning another charity ball.'

'God forbid!'

She laughed with him. 'Well, my mother thinks it'll be the event of the summer, and it'll keep Wanda busy for a while.' Her mother also thought she was a fool for loving this man.

He said sardonically, 'I suppose that's a mercy. Any other news?'

She would not talk to him about the hotel. It was a topic that always seemed to be tense between them. She smoothed the upholstery of the sofa with her free hand. 'My brother called and he's met the most wonderful woman in the Maritimes. My mother's worried that he'll get married back there and she'll miss the chance to pull off a social coup.'

'What does your brother say?'

She pulled her legs up beside her. 'He wants a wedding, not a circus, and she's a small-town girl so Mom can go find another event to organise.'

'Good for your brother.'

'I was rather pleased with him. He's grown up well, I think . . .' And he'd fallen in love with a girl who loved him back. She bit her lip. 'What about Elizabeth Lake? What's up there?'

'Melting snow. Your aunt had another tea party last night.'

'Oh, lord.' She closed her eyes. 'What's wrong now? Are they lynching her?'

'Not so far as I know.' So that wasn't why he'd called. 'I heard about it from Mary Anne, who went, and she said it was a lark and half the irate mothers were there too.'

Sarah laughed and curled her hand around her ankle. 'Well, let me know if violence erupts. How's Casey?'

'He chased a porcupine and got a mouthful of quills. Dad and I took them out and now Casey is thinking twice when he hears sounds in the trees.'

'Poor Casey. Give him a hug for me.' For a moment she thought she'd lost the connection, then his voice came, husky and low.

'Sarah, come away with me this weekend.'

Her heart stopped. Could she get away for an entire weekend? There was that convention, and Justin who kept insisting on a meeting.

'Yes,' she whispered. 'Where?'

'I'll surprise you.'

She laughed, warmth and hope bubbling in her veins. 'What do I bring? A ball-gown or a winter parka?'

'Blue jeans and trainers and a jacket in case the wind comes up. It's spring, green sprouting everywhere, but you never know. I'll pick you up Friday afternoon at four. All right?'

'I'll be ready,' she promised, although she knew that she would have a terrible job to organise things so that she could go. She would have to go down to her office tonight and start working towards getting free.

Every time Alex came to Vancouver he left her aching with frustration and facing an increasingly difficult job at the hotel. She knew that her control over the perpetual chaos of running the hotel was slipping. Her accountant and her lawyer knew, too, and she suspected that soon Justin would have a talk with her about duty and responsibility and the mire of troubles waiting for a hotel owner who let her attention slip.

She didn't know what to do about it. She had no idea what kept Alex coming to see her, but felt instinctively that it was fragile. He was good company, humorous and even-tempered, but he did not like talking about her hotel. They discussed her family and his, the theatre and the latest bestsellers. Sometimes they talked about Elizabeth Lake, sometimes about politics. Except for the night of the charity ball, they almost never talked about Stellers Gardens.

Each time Alex came to Vancouver he made demands on her time that were increasingly difficult for Sarah to manage. She was afraid to tell him how difficult it was becoming. She had a sick conviction that if she started putting him off she would never see him again.

A weekend. A whole weekend. That would be the worst.

CHAPTER NINE

AT FIRST it seemed that everything would co-operate to let Sarah be free for the weekend. Through the week Sarah and Brenda worked through a ream of paperwork and Sarah did everything she could to allow for complications over the weekend.

On Friday morning she told Brenda, 'If the chef needs extra help for that convention banquet, call Edgar in right away. He's carrying a pager, and I'm paying him stand-by for the weekend, so don't hesitate.'

'I won't,' promised Brenda. 'You said you had to go out shopping.'

'In a minute.' What disaster had she failed to provide for? She chewed on her lip, wondering if she could get Alex to give her a contact number that she could leave Brenda. She always left a contact if she was going to be gone for more than a few hours.

'If that lift breaks down again——'

'I know, Sarah, and so does maintenance. If you don't go shopping for those jeans you'll never make it! You've got the accountant in an hour, then the lawyer.'

'Right, I'm going now.' Crazy that she didn't have a pair of jeans, but her life demanded businesslike tailoring and impeccable grooming. Jeans and a sweatshirt didn't fit in, but she thought they sounded delightfully frivolous.

A whole weekend, just casual clothes and Alex.

She went by taxi, hurriedly. She bought two pairs of jeans, two casual blouses and a sweatshirt, then topped her purchases off with a pair of Nikes and managed to get back to the office just as Warren was coming in.

'I'll be right in,' she told the accountant as she handed the bags to Brenda. 'Send those up to my room, would you, Brenda?'

'Should I have someone from housekeeping get the labels and such off?'

'Right,' agreed Sarah, grinning because it was only a few hours now and Alex would be downstairs with the limousine, waiting for her. She said gaily, 'I'd look a fool with labels hanging everywhere. And have I told you, Brenda, how wonderfully efficient you are?'

She went in to the accountant, pleased when his weekly report was brief enough for Sarah to get him out of her office before lunch. She watched him leaving, thinking that Alex had been wrong when he'd told her that the hotel was running her. A weekend off, and she was managing it reasonably smoothly. Quite efficiently, in fact, and her staff would be fine while she was gone two days, even if she couldn't find a telephone to check back.

'Lunch with Justin,' Brenda reminded her. 'Twenty minutes from now, in the garden-room.'

'I'll be there.'

First she took time to stop off in her room, where the new clothes were laid out neatly on her bed with her overnight bag beside them. Someone had begun to pack for her. She opened it and saw a toilet bag with toothbrush and toothpaste inside, a selection of make-up in the side-pocket. Two changes of lingerie. Brenda's doing, Sarah decided thankfully.

Sarah sorted through her purchases and added one pair of the jeans and the sweatshirt to the bag. Then she put in the nightgown that she had bought three weeks ago in response to a heated fantasy of Alex knocking on the door of her suite. In the fantasy she had gone

slowly to the door, her body throbbing with anticipation...then the door, opening...Alex, coming inside,
reaching for her...going into his arms...his voice, low
and shaken, whispering that he loved her forever.

Fantasy because the reality had been this strange series
of platonic meetings, slow conversation with moments
of incredible emotional intimacy. And tension.

She added one of the blouses to the bag, then realised
that she'd forgotten a jacket. Luckily, her ski jacket was
here and not at Mother's. She laid that beside the jeans
and blouse which she planned to wear to meet Alex.
Jeans, he'd told her, so she would wear jeans, and if the
staff gave her strange looks she didn't care.

She had forgotten socks for the Nikes. She packed
tights instead. Did Alex intend this weekend to be two
days truly together, the way she dreamed? She ached for
the tension to be gone between them, yearned to touch
his shoulder instead of always holding back that impulse, to lean back in the circle of his arm and close her
eyes and feel music playing somewhere as they sat in
front of the fire.

Her telephone buzzed. Brenda, reminding her that it
was time for lunch with Justin. Sarah dashed down to
the restaurant.

'Sorry,' she gasped when Justin rose to greet her.
'Sorry I'm late.'

He murmured, 'You're always worth waiting for,
Sarah.' Which was crazy because she was never late for
her appointments with him.

She sat down, mentally going through the other things
that had to be done before she could escape for a whole
weekend. Check with housekeeping and bookings
and...what else?

They ordered without looking at the menu. Sarah took
the special because she wanted to check whether it was

over-spiced as a guest had complained earlier. She sighed and wished for the millionth time that she could simply walk away from the details of Stellers Gardens. Justin was going on about the company's annual general meeting, wanting her to set a date to discuss the agenda.

'Next week,' she said. 'Set our discussion up for Wednesday or Thursday and give Brenda the time.'

'Friday would be better for me.'

'No, not Friday.'

'Sarah, Friday is really best for me.' He frowned. 'We always meet on Fridays.'

'I have plans.' She didn't, not yet, but Alex might ask her to go away for another weekend.

He shrugged in irritation. 'All right, then. I'll try for Wednesday.' He made a note in the little black book he always carried. 'Now, about those new employee contracts.'

The business lunch with Justin lasted until one-thirty. After that Sarah had just enough time to get the house-keeping manager into her office, followed by the bookings manager. Then she hurriedly began clearing up her telephone messages.

Brenda came in an endless time later, harried and slightly flushed. 'It's the conventions, Sarah. They want their meeting-rooms changed. They need another one, they say, and——' Brenda waved a sheaf of papers '—Dr Mudge, the convention co-ordinator, insists you talk with him personally.'

Not this weekend. Please! Not *this* weekend! Sarah bit her lip, knowing that she should cancel her weekend with Alex. How could she leave when there was a major convention going on inside the hotel? Sarah felt nausea welling up.

'I'd better stay. With this going on, I can't leave.'

Brenda wailed, 'Sarah, don't cancel! You've looked so alive since you started seeing him again, and you've hardly had more than a few hours at a time away from here. Just settle Dr Mudge, then leave.' Brenda frowned. 'But I would feel better if I had a number where I could reach you if all hell breaks loose.'

'I'll call you,' she promised Brenda. Somehow she would find a telephone and then, if she had to come back, she'd come back. But she would have tonight with Alex first, at the very least.

Brenda said with a grin, 'Well, you can wait until tomorrow to call. After all, what could you accomplish in the middle of the night?' She flushed and Sarah did too, mostly because Brenda's imagination of what went on between Sarah and Alex had to be a lot more heated than the reality these last few weeks.

'It's twenty to four,' Brenda warned her.

Alex would be waiting downstairs at four.

'All right. Tell Dr Mudge he can have the Twilight Room until tomorrow night. I'll call you tomorrow.' Her father would tell her that it was completely irresponsible for her to leave the hotel now, but if she went down and told Alex she couldn't go she might never see him again.

Maybe she could explain, ask him to stay with her this weekend. They could take the penthouse suite in the towers, and she'd tell Brenda no calls, nothing unless it was truly urgent.

No.

Sarah fled to her private room and dressed hurriedly in jeans and trainers and a silky blouse that was technically casual but Sarah thought Alex would find it—well, maybe seductive. 'Come away,' he had asked, and the one time she had suggested he come here to her suite he had refused at once. Whatever he planned for the weekend, he would not accept hiding away in the Stellers Gardens towers as a substitute.

She caught up her ski jacket and the bulging overnight bag. She had over-packed for just a weekend. Out in the corridor she pushed the lift button and waited, but she could see the indicator up on the eleventh floor and it seemed to be staying there. She frowned, wondering why, then it moved and it was going up, not down. The other two lifts seemed firmly anchored down at the lobby level, according to the lighted displays over them.

If she was late, would Alex wait?

She turned and pushed the door to the fire stairs open, then ran down and out into the lobby. The doorman momentarily looked startled at the sight of the boss flying out of the front door in jeans and Nikes. She stopped on the tarmac, feeing the pain well up because there was no limousine and he hadn't waited.

Alex . . .

'Ms Stellers! This way.'

She saw him then. He was there, dressed casually in jeans and a rib-knit sweater over an open-necked shirt, reaching out a hand to draw her towards him.

'Sorry I'm late!' she gasped, still breathless from her rush down the stairs.

'Worth every second of the wait,' he murmured.

He guided her into the front passenger-seat of the dark blue BMW she had seen in his garage back in January. She sat inside the car with her cheeks flushing while he put her overnight bag in the boot. 'Worth every second,' he had said, and there had been something shattering in his voice.

He slipped into the driver's seat, smiling the lazy smile that haunted her nights. 'All set?' he asked. 'Here, let me throw that jacket in the back. You won't need it inside the car.'

She handed him the jacket and fastened her seatbelt, the flush returning to her face as he swept his gaze over her. 'I like that blouse,' he said, his eyes clinging to the way it caressed the curves of her breast.

'Thanks,' she whispered.

He was smiling as he drove away from the hotel.

'You brought the car down here?' she asked unnecessarily, needing to hear his voice.

'Hmm,' he agreed, slowing just enough to catch the green light as it changed. He was a better driver than most of the limousine drivers they'd had. He said, 'It doesn't suit Elizabeth Lake very well, anyway, but I couldn't make myself get rid of it when I left Toronto.'

She smiled slightly. A four-wheel drive truck for the snow-drifts, and a city car that was sleek and fast and filled with luxury. Two different men, or maybe a dozen men, but she was starting to feel sometimes that she knew most of them.

'You drove down yourself?' she asked.

He nodded, and she didn't realise that she was still smiling until he stopped at a light and reached across to trace the curve of her lips. 'What's this, Sarah? Do you like the thought of my spending twenty hours on the road?'

'It surely didn't take twenty hours in this car?' His lips twitched and her heart sang. Something in the way he looked at her softened the tension that she felt she had lived with forever. She whispered, 'What I like is the thought of your driving all that way just to see me.' She touched her flaming cheeks and finished weakly, 'I— that was a silly thing to say.'

'Was it?' He must not have minded because he was smiling as he moved with the heavy Friday traffic towards the drive through Stanley Park. She smoothed her hands along the new crispness of her jeans and felt herself relaxing a little more.

'We're going over Lions Gate bridge?' she speculated.

He grinned and teased, 'Are you sure? Maybe I'm taking you for a week in Stanley Park.'

She felt warmth because it was the kind of thing a real lover might do, teasing the woman he loved with a pleasant surprise. She hazarded, 'North Vancouver? West Vancouver?' but he just smiled and she said, 'You're not going to tell me, are you?'

'No. You might decide you don't want to come.'

'Might I?' If he believed that, he saw less of her thoughts than she had believed.

He said quietly, 'This weekend is an experiment we're going to make.'

An experiment. She chewed on her lower lip, wondering what he meant. She could feel her tension crawling back. She glanced at Alex and he seemed relaxed, but he almost always did.

'Alex?'

'Hmm?' He glanced at her, then back to the road. They had crossed the old Lions Gate suspension bridge and were driving through the downtown area of West Vancouver now.

She twisted a strand of hair around her index finger. 'I try to picture you as head of that Toronto brokerage sometimes, and all I can imagine is you completely in control of it, not getting harried and rushed. And— you've made scathing comments about my being in the rat race. I just wondered—well, if you had some way of managing it that——' She spread her hands helplessly. 'I just have trouble picturing you letting anything get control of you that you didn't want to.'

'Use your imagination,' he said wryly.

'You never seem to get uptight.'

'Never?'

She flushed, remembering the night they had made love, remembering his voice, harsh and driven, trying to make her leave when he discovered that she was completely inexperienced. And the night of the Cassidy ball, when she had felt the wires of his tension drawing tight inside herself.

'Alex, the night of Wanda Cassidy's ball—did you come to Vancouver just to see me?'

He merged on to the Upper Levels highway, westbound, before he answered, 'Yes. I had to see you again.'

He wasn't going to say any more, but Sarah hugged those words to her. He'd *had* to see her again, and he might tell himself that it was only an affair that would end, but he hadn't believed it any more than she did.

They came down the hill and into the ferry queue for Langdale. 'The Sunshine Coast?' she speculated.

'Impatient, aren't you?'

'Yes,' she agreed, sobered. She was impatient and, as he'd said more than once, a workaholic. He accomplished a lot more than she did, but he had a knack for doing it without getting himself involved. It frightened her because he might deal with having an affair with a woman the same way. This affair, with her. Sometimes, she felt that she was beginning to understand him and sometimes she felt . . . just scared.

On the ferry Alex took her outside and they stood at the rail in the spring sunshine. When he put his arm around her she felt something warming inside, a nameless fear fading. It was going to be all right.

On the other side the road up British Columbia's little strip of Sunshine Coast was narrow and twisting. Alex took the branch that bypassed the small town of Gibsons and Sarah didn't ask exactly where they were going. It would be some little resort and very quiet because it wasn't really tourist season yet. 'An experiment,' he had said, and he was taking her somewhere where they would be quiet and alone, with no interruptions.

She pushed aside her mother's warning about men who would never let the ghost of an old love go. He must care, more than just a casual affair. When he took her out of that society ball it would have been easy to carry on from where she'd run out of his bedroom back in Elizabeth Lake, drowning in the heat until it—until it burned out for him. He had told her that was what he planned, but it wasn't what had happened. Instead Alex had deliberately slowed down the pace of their relationship over the last weeks.

He pulled off the road just before a steep hill, taking a narrow branch down towards the water. He drove the twisted private lane through trees and a tall hedge, then into a car park, where there was no sign of any house or cottage.

He turned off the engine and Sarah didn't wait for him to help her out. She was out of the door and going to the edge of a cliff, hanging on to the rail and looking down at the house that had been hidden until she'd got to the edge. It was by the water, someone's hideaway. Alex touched her shoulder and she turned.

'Are we staying here?'

'Yes.' He was watching her, searching for something in her eyes. 'We'll stay here until Monday morning.'

She swallowed, thankful that she had been evasive about commitments for Monday morning when she had gone over next week's appointments with Brenda.

'Any problem with that, Sarah?' There was a hint of coolness in the question.

'No. No problem.' She moved ahead of him, down the stairs towards the small holiday home, asking, 'Is this another of your places? An apartment in Vancouver, a home in Elizabeth Lake. Is there something in Toronto, too? And this?'

'In Toronto, yes.' His voice was cool and she wondered what had happened to the easy warmth between them. He said, 'I borrowed this cottage from Charles for the weekend.'

She remarked stiffly, 'I didn't know Charles had a summer home. Come to that, I've never heard of Charles Kantos actually taking a holiday.'

'He hardly ever uses it.' Alex's voice was muffled as he bent to unlock the door. 'Charles owns all the trappings of the good life, but he's married to his work.'

'Yes,' Sarah agreed mechanically. She had seen Charles at various functions over the years. He did not dance, seldom stayed late unless he was talking to quiet, powerful men, and then it was probably business. When Sarah saw him with a woman, the woman was usually beautiful, and temporary. Playing wasn't something Charles did much of, and, when he did, Sarah suspected that business still had first place.

So if this was Charles's summer place there would be a telephone to keep in touch. Sarah worried her lower lip as she waited for Alex to unlock the door. She almost wished that Alex had brought her somewhere where she had no choice, no telephone, no way to call the hotel. She would have to call and leave Brenda the number, and hope that whatever happened over the weekend didn't require that she return.

Inside the cottage was a simple, breathless magic. She walked past Alex to where a clever architect had made an entire wall into a window on the ocean. There were houses all along this bay, but somehow the architect had placed the building such that Sarah could only see the rocks and water and the evergreen trees that rose up towards the sky. She and Alex were alone in the universe, with only the slowly surging ocean outside lapping on the dock.

'Sarah...'

His hands were on her shoulders and she held her breath, staring out and seeing nothing, every nerve in her body poised for his faintest touch. His hands moved into her hair and she felt the pins coming out and thought she heard something soft, as if he was pulling each one out slowly and letting it drop. She closed her eyes and his fingers searched through her hair, finding the last pin and letting the curly confusion free to tumble down her shoulders.

'That's better,' he whispered. 'I've been wanting to do that for weeks.'

'Why didn't you?' she whispered.

His hands explored the softness of her curls, slowly spread her hair to riot over her shoulders. Then he slid his fingers over the silky contours of her blouse and she heard her own breath, a long drink of air taken in with the rising tension from his caressing fingers.

'It's like unwrapping presents,' he said soberly. 'Sometimes a man doesn't know if he's ready for what's inside.'

She touched the muscle that moved along his jaw. 'What——?'

'I brought the BMW down because I thought it would be more convenient.' He was frowning. 'Because I intend to keep seeing you, and I may as well have a car if I'm going to spend a portion of my life in Vancouver.'

'A...portion?' Sarah bit her lip to keep from asking— did he mean a portion of his life forever?

He traced the boundaries of her curls with both hands, lightly stroking the irregular edge that caressed the upper slopes of her breasts. 'I had dinner packed for us. It's in a basket in the trunk of the BMW. Cold dinner, but the chef assures me it would tempt the gods. I'll go out and get it.'

'All right,' she whispered, wondering why she felt a sad pain at his words, and knew the answer. He had put a definite boundary on Sarah's place in his life. Part of his life. Here and in Vancouver. But they would live apart.

When she heard the door close she moved quickly to search for the telephone. There was one in the kitchen, but he would be back in a minute and could easily catch her calling. Not that there was any reason she shouldn't. He must realise that she couldn't just go incommunicado. He was a businessman himself, and . . .

She found an extension in the bedroom and dialled quickly, keying in her calling-card number when the tone went, then, when the hotel answered, asking, 'Is Brenda Hilton in?'

Brenda did not respond when the desk paged her. Sarah left a message and the telephone number of Charles Kantos's summer home. Only in an emergency, and why should there be any emergency?

She put the phone back down and opened her bag. Alex had brought it into the bedroom. It was sitting beside his, and she had known of course what a weekend together meant, but her fingers were trembling as she put her things into the empty drawers of the dresser. She kept glancing in the mirror and seeing the massive expanse of the big bed reflected there.

What would it be like, waking in the morning with his arms around her? Would he hold her all night as he had the night when he first taught her to need him? Would he smile at her in the morning when she opened her eyes.

She was brushing her hair when he came into the room. 'Do you want me to unpack your things?' she asked.

'I'll do that.' He moved behind her, their eyes meeting in the mirror as he took the brush from her hand and said in a husky voice, 'I'll do that, too,' and began to stroke the brush down through her hair in slow, seductive strokes.

She would have closed her eyes, drowning in the pleasure of this strangely intimate caress, but his gaze held hers in the mirror and she was still staring, watching his face as he concentrated on brushing the wildness of her hair into long, soft waves. Then he put the brush down.

She turned around very slowly.

He told her huskily, 'This is how I dream of you. Standing in front of me. Your hair everywhere, and your eyes...' He reached towards her and slowly unfastened the button just below her throat. Then the next button. He said harshly, 'Your aunt came to my office wearing that sweater... the sweater you were wearing the night we made love.'

She tried to say something. Her throat was dry and frozen. She looked down and his hands were loosening the next button. She wanted to reach up and touch his face because it was filled with tenderness that made her heart catch.

'I borrowed the sweater,' she said finally. 'I sent it back to her after I got...home to Vancouver. And I dream about you, too, all the time. I—can I come back some time? To Elizabeth Lake?' To you, she meant, but hadn't the courage to say those words. Alex had put boundaries on their relationship.

'You can come.' His voice sounded sombre. His hands were almost brisk on the last button. 'Casey's been asking after you. And your aunt——'

'My aunt?'

He shook his head and stepped back, touching her cheek and bringing her eyes up so that he could meet her gaze. 'Our supper's waiting,' he said quietly, and it was a question.

'You've been undressing me.' She smiled slightly. 'Do you want me to...change for dinner?'

'You know damn well what I want, Sarah!' He moved closer, his thumbs grazing her flesh gently as he pushed the blouse back and the silky stuff slipped down her arms. 'I want you. I've wanted you for a long time.'

She lifted her lips and he took them, catching her close so that she gasped with the hard need of his body and the aching response of hers. 'I've wanted you, too,' she whispered, and then there was nothing she could say at all because her breath was gone and her heart was thundering as he swept her into his arms and carried her towards the big bed.

CHAPTER TEN

'I WANT to tell you about my marriage.'

Sarah froze. She had been sitting in Alex's arms in the big sofa, staring into the fire and dreaming while he stroked her hair and murmured words that made her feel soft and warm and loved.

They had been at the Sunshine Coast hideaway for just over twenty-four hours. Sarah had never in her life felt so incredibly happy and fulfilled. She had decided that she felt exactly the way a woman should feel when she loved a man who looked at her the way Alex did.

'Your...wife?' She closed her eyes and whispered, 'All right,' knowing that she didn't want to hear this. 'Beautiful,' her mother had said, 'and brilliant.' Alex had loved his wife so deeply that her death had torn the fabric of his life forever.

'We were married for four years.'

Sarah was thankful that Alex had started this when she was staring into the fire, when he could not see her face and she could not see his.

'She was assistant manager of a Scarborough bank when we got married.' He was twisting her hair around his fingers. Had Denise had long, waving hair? Was that why he kept touching her hair? She had thought it was for her, for caring and sharing.

She asked painfully, 'Did she look like me?'

'No, not looks.' She thought he shrugged and that hurt even though she didn't understand the gesture. He said, 'After we married she changed banks to take a manager's position in downtown Toronto.'

161

She swallowed. He was talking about things that did not matter. Talking about his wife's job because he could not bear to talk about the woman herself, to remember the personal things, even after three years.

'I spent most of our marriage building up the brokerage.' Sarah thought that the movement she felt was another shrug. 'Successfully, but no, Sarah, I was not a cool, laid-back stockbroker. If you'd asked me then I'd have told you that running in high gear accomplished more, made me feel alive.' He tugged on her hair and then released it. 'I was heavily into accomplishments. So was Denise.'

He was going to tell her how much he loved Denise, and Sarah wasn't sure that she could trust her own reactions. She should listen and be sympathetic. Anything else would be barbaric because it was a tragedy when a beautiful, brilliant woman died. The woman Alex loved.

She felt a scream building up inside.

He twisted another of her curls, then released it and she felt him smoothing her hair. 'We were what you would call an upwardly mobile couple. Everyone said we were perfect for each other, and, if pairing two ambitious workaholics is a good match, then we were.'

She whispered, 'I don't understand.'

'When she died——'

She had to turn then, to see him. She captured his hands and said quietly, 'I know you left Toronto because of her. I know you're still grieving for her.' She closed her eyes and added harshly, 'I know I can't take her place.'

'No one knows why I left. No one but me.'

She froze. 'Why?'

'Because of all the things I *didn't* feel.' He brought her back into his arms. 'When Denise died I realised that I didn't know her at all. We'd been married four years, been engaged two, and spent most of that time re-scheduling the wedding because of her job or mine.' He stroked her arm absently. 'We both worked seven day weeks and when she was gone I realised we'd been room-mates, not husband and wife.'

He tightened his arms around her. 'It shook me up when I lost her, yes. But mostly I felt guilty that I'd lived with a woman for four years and she might as well have been a stranger. Guilty, because after her death I missed the routine, the habits we'd built up in our tear-around life a lot more than I missed the woman . . . her smile or her hair or her laugh.'

'You must have been in love when you married her.'

He said wryly, 'Compatible, I suppose, and getting married seemed a sensible thing to do. I guess I had some idea of a family some time, but I don't know if she saw that. We were both too damned busy to take time to do a decent job of making a marriage.' He twisted another curl around and around until she could feel the tension in her scalp from the pulling. 'We would have gone on that way, and I'd have got to somewhere in my forties and started asking myself what the hell my life was about. Or maybe she would have left me before that happened, because, when I try to look into the inside of our relationship, there was nothing there. Denise's death was a tragedy, a young and talented woman losing her life, and sad, because I realised she was my wife but she was a stranger.'

He released her hair again, smoothed both hands down along her arms. 'I left Toronto because I wanted more out of the rest of my life. I enjoy the stock market. It's a challenge, and I'm good at it. But I didn't want to come to the end of my life with nothing but a portfolio. Like Charles, amassing land and money, but he has no private life. That was me, except that technically I had a family.' He half sighed and said, 'After Denise died you might say I went looking for the rest of Alex Candon because I didn't much like the man I knew.'

Sarah caught his hands and felt his chest strong against her back, his arms surrounding her. 'The stockbroker?'

'And Denise's husband. I wasn't much of a husband, bad enough that I didn't even know what was missing between us.' He held her closer. 'I wanted time to go outside and smell the seasons, time to keep an eye on Kelly, who's growing so damned fast and is a great kid, but going through a restless stage. Time to keep tabs on the market, too, and I've managed that better than I'd thought I could. But I've learned that I need all the rest, too, Sarah. Being closer to nature, having time for people.'

There was tension in him now. 'I told myself that if I became seriously involved with another woman she would be someone who wanted to live the same way. I wanted a home and a family and time for loving.' His arms clenched in a spasm of muscles and he said, 'Either that, or nothing.'

She closed her eyes and felt the flames warming her all the way from the fireplace, and wondered what he would say now if she said that she loved him, if she said that she wanted all the things he wanted—except that she was trapped in the world he had vowed to keep clear of.

'Sarah——'

The telephone rang into the silence of his hesitation. She felt him stiffening and she gasped, 'Don't answer it! Don't——'

He bent to press a kiss against her cheek, but she couldn't see his face. 'I'll just be a minute. Charles is the only one who knows we're here, and it'll be some-

thing crazy, like telling us where he keeps his wine or
how to turn on the hot water.'

She protested, 'But we got the water on——' But he
was walking away and it was no use at all. She heard
his voice and she knew that she should follow because
it was going to be the hotel and he would know that he
had been right in the first place—their affair was going
to be a disaster.

He came back into the living-room. 'It's for you.'

She stood up, her hand pushing through her hair, her
eyes pleading for understanding. 'I had to call Brenda,
to leave a number.'

'Of course.' He understood, and his eyes were cynical.
'So go and talk to her, because she's waiting.'

She gulped and got past him and Brenda screamed in
her ear, 'Sarah! You've got to get back here! It's that
lift they overhauled last week! Between the tenth and
eleventh floor, and it's jammed! Maintenance say it could
take twelve hours to get it free, and Dr Mudge is on the
emergency phone from the lift, threatening to sue us.
There's fire engines outside—no fire, but I don't know—
the fire chief said something about using the ladders.
And Justin—he says you'd better be here to talk to
Mudge when he gets out of the lift.'

Sarah shuddered. 'You mean he's in it?'

'Yes, and...oh, lord, Sarah! What should I do?'

'Hold on a minute.' Alex was standing in the doorway
to the living-room, watching her with his jaw rigid and
his eyes disillusioned or something even harsher. Her
voice was brittle as she asked, 'Alex, can I—is there any
way I can get back tonight?'

He glanced at his watch and said coldly, 'Why not?
If you cut the phone call short I can get you to the last
ferry.'

He turned and walked away while she was assuring Brenda that she would be there as soon as she could. 'Tonight. It'll depend somewhat on what the traffic's like coming into the city from the ferry terminal, but—as soon as I can.'

Alex wasn't in the living-room. She heard sounds and he was in the bedroom, pushing things into his bag. She opened the drawers and took her things out, crammed them in. He was folding and packing tidily, but she just shoved everything of hers into the bag. She opened her mouth once to explain to him, but it was no use trying to tell him how urgent it was, how she had no choice. There would always be something urgent in her life. An irate and prominent doctor stuck in a lift, or flooding in the basement. This would happen again and again and it was exactly what Alex would not allow in his life.

He had learned to put people first, before work, and he wasn't willing to have less from the woman in his life. She loved him desperately, but she didn't know how to get free for him. She understood now that it would never work between them unless she could. Being Alex's Vancouver lover was a very small, isolated place that he seemed willing to make for her in his life, but she would never have more than that because she couldn't come to him free and able to give all of herself.

'Done with that?' he asked when she zipped it.

She handed him the bag and he turned and walked out with both bags, and tossed back, 'Better hurry or you'll miss that ferry.'

He seemed determined to get her there, to be rid of her. They drove to the terminal in silence, got out of the car together on the ferry and went up to the lounge, where he left her while he went into the news-stand. He came back with the *Globe,* which he read while she tried not to cry.

When the announcement for docking came over the loudspeaker they went back to the car silently. It was raining when Alex drove off the ferry. A dismal evening, rain and city lights under a dark sky. He navigated the ferry off-loading and speeded up as he came out on to the highway towards Vancouver. He shifted lanes and began to pass a big transport truck.

She said quietly, 'I was engaged a few years ago.'

'Charles told me.' He didn't sound very interested.

She swallowed and drew her knees up, hugging them close to her and staring out of the windscreen. 'His name was Kevin. He was an engineer, worked for a consulting company that built power stations here and there around the world.'

He was listening, she supposed, but he didn't even glance at her. He was driving fast, passing the ferry traffic that had come off the boat ahead of them and working his way steadily out into the empty highway ahead of the other cars and trucks.

She said doggedly, 'We got engaged when I was twenty-four, just before my father died. I was working in the hotel, assistant manager, and—Kevin was going out to Jakarta to build this hydroelectric dam.'

Alex moved down a gear as he came up behind a van pulling a utility trailer.

Sarah said, 'Then my father died, and someone had to look after the hotel and the family—my kid brother and my mother and Aunt Lori because she was pretty strange after the—— My uncle, you see, died in that plane crash with my father. It was a private plane and...you already know about that.'

He passed the van and she stared through its window at the silhouette of a bearded man and a woman. She said, 'I had to take over.'

Alex replied, 'Of course.'

She closed her eyes and hugged her legs closer. He turned off the highway and they were coming down through the bit of downtown New Westminster before the Lions Gate bridge. Soon he would be at the hotel.

They went through the lights without speaking. Alex merged left and started up the slope of the bridge. Outside the rain made everything shiny in the headlights.

On top of the bridge she said, 'Kevin agreed that we had to put off the wedding, but the months kept going on and when it came time to go to Jakarta he said I had to choose; marry him or run the hotel because he wasn't waiting ten years for me to get free. Or forever, he said, because that's how long it would be.'

Alex geared down as the BMW floated towards the dark mass of Stanley Park's trees. Through the park and into the core of the city, and when he pulled into the valet parking area in front of the hotel it would be the end.

Alex said, 'You chose the hotel.'

'Yes,' she agreed miserably. There hadn't been any choice. She wondered if it would do any good to tell him that she would find a way, that she'd force the family to agree to put it on the market, except that prices had dropped through the floor last year.

He was on Georgia Street now and she said quietly, 'So he left and it wasn't a lot different from you and Denise, except we never got married, but I didn't have time to miss him and mostly I felt sad because I'd wanted . . . because I don't suppose I was that much in love with him.' She closed her eyes tightly as Alex went through the last green light. All the lights were green for him tonight and there was hardly any traffic. The city had already fled for the weekend and the downtown core was quiet.

When he turned and went up the slight hill to the valet parking area he asked grimly, 'Is there a point to this?'

She gulped and he stopped and she said painfully, 'Just that—that nothing has really changed and you're right, I don't have time for—for a relationship and I guess this will keep happening over and over again and——' She gulped and stared at the uniform of the man coming to open the door and let her out. Behind him were two firemen talking together. Would they have got Dr Mudge out of the lift by ladder from above? She could not imagine the pudgy doctor climbing a ladder.

Alex's voice was toneless. 'So it would be best if we forgot the whole thing? Didn't see each other again?'

She swallowed a sob. 'I guess . . . that would be best.'

The passenger door opened. Sarah got out and the doorman had her arm, helping her up and holding an umbrella over her head while Alex got out her bag and handed it to him.

'Goodbye,' he said.

She met his eyes and there was nothing there. Just grey nothing, like a fading field of snow. 'Goodbye,' she whispered and she wanted to go into his arms, to beg him to want whatever she could manage to offer him, but he was turning away and she let the doorman guide her towards the doors.

As she heard the suppressed roar of the BMW leaving the doorman murmured to her, 'Miss Hilton says Dr Mudge is in your office.'

Sarah swallowed the pain. 'Have the desk call to say I'll be there in ten minutes, as soon as I've changed.'

Kevin had given her his ultimatum in her father's office, in this same hotel. Her father's office had been hers by that time, but she had still thought of it as his. She remembered watching Kevin leave, knowing there was no calling him back.

Only a pale echo of what she felt as she listened to the sound of Alex's car leaving her forever. She had been busy in the days after Kevin left, thankful that the need to work left no time for pain or sadness. After a while, she had realised that there was no pain, that it had slipped away without her knowing.

Unfortunately, in the days after Alex left, the hectic pace of hotel life did nothing to deaden Sarah's pain. Once the lift emergency was over the hotel conducted its hospitality calmly. Dr Mudge was irate, but Sarah and Justin managed, together, to calm him down with a promise of a major discount on the hotel bill.

On Wednesday Justin passed on a letter that he had received from another lawyer. Sarah stared at it in shock.

'Someone's making an offer to buy Stellers shares? How? We're not listed.'

Justin shrugged. 'A private purchase. It would take an expert valuation to determine if that's a fair price, since you're not listed. I can't imagine how they came up with a price at all without a look at your books.'

'They? Who?' Sarah stared at the words of the brief lawyer's letter. 'There's no mention of who the buyer would be.'

'Probably a hotel chain.' He named the major chain which did not have a hotel in downtown Vancouver.

'I——'

Sarah closed her lips, pushing back a dream of the whole mess taken off her shoulders and herself in Alex's arms. Alex hadn't even suggested she try to get out of the hotel, probably thought that she was so deeply in-grained in her rat race life that she would never change even if the hotel evaporated. Heaven knew, he might be right. She had never had the chance to find out if she could live any other way.

Justin picked up his briefcase. 'I'll reply, shall I? Tell them no? On your behalf, that is. The offer has to be presented to the other shareholders as well. Your mother, your brother. And your aunt.'

She could escape her bondage if she wanted. The offer was contingent on acquisition of fifty-one per cent of the shares. That meant mother and Mike and Aunt Lori, or enough to constitute fifty-one per cent.

She shook her head, feeling dizzy and slightly disorientated. 'Of course we can't sell, give up control.' She felt weak suddenly. If Alex . . . but it was too late for that now. 'I—don't say no yet.'

Justin's eyes narrowed. 'Are you considering selling?'

She went to the window and stared out. She whispered, 'I've dreamed of being free...' but knew that there might not be any hope for her and Alex now because the last time she saw him their parting had been very final. She had destroyed it when she took that phone call from Brenda. Even before that it had been terribly fragile because he had never once said the word love.

'Justin, what do you think of the offer?'

He sighed and stood up, getting ready to leave because he had other work to do. He said, 'It's more difficult all the time to go it alone in this business. You're doing well, but it won't get easier. Interest rates could be up again in the summer, they say, and—it's easier for a big chain with a world-wide booking set-up. We could get a valuation. There seems to be some willingness to negotiate price and terms, up to a point.'

'My father would hate to see us sell.'

'Your father's gone, Sarah. It's not his decision. It's yours.'

When Justin was gone Sarah told Brenda, 'I'm going to my room for a while. Unless it's urgent . . .'

'Right,' agreed Brenda. 'Unless we get a hysterical guest who needs to be brought back to earth with that cool stare of yours, I'll keep everything away from you. Do you want a meal sent up?'

She shook her head. If she tried to eat she would choke. Did she have a cool stare? It didn't sound like the kind of thing a man would want in a woman he loved. But then, Alex had never said he loved her, just that he wanted her. He had made it perfectly clear that Sarah did not fit his image of the ideal woman.

Sarah sighed and went down to the lobby in the lift. She walked through the reception area, past the concierge and into the quiet television lounge. She wasn't sure why she was here. Perhaps she was simply wandering, looking at it all, wondering if she *could* be free, if there was any chance to bring Alex back into her life.

There were two businessmen in here, talking in low voices. The television on the wall was turned down, a muted version of the news just under the level of the men's voices. Sarah saw a flash of evergreen trees on the television screen, heard snatches of words from the wind-blown news reporter who was going on about a search.

Her heart stopped with a painful crash. *Where* had that report come from?

A missing helicopter?

Alex?

The two men turned to stare at her. She must have gasped aloud, or perhaps Alex's name had escaped her lips. On the television the scene had changed. Sarah turned, stumbling out of the lounge and into the newly replaced lift. Automatically she pushed the button for the floor which her office was on.

Brenda had the radio on low in her office. Sarah caught a few words just as her assistant looked up and said, 'Sarah? I thought you—what's wrong?'

'What were they saying on the news? What's that about a search? They said a helicopter, didn't they? Where?'

'A missing helicopter.' Brenda nodded. 'Crashed, north of Smithers. It—Sarah?'

Sarah staggered into her office and closed the door behind her. Of course it wasn't him. There had to be hundreds of helicopters in the north and Alex was the kind of man who kept control of whatever he did. His affairs. His vehicles. His life.

Accidents happened, even to careful people.

She fumbled the buttons on her phone and had to dial twice. She called his house and there was no answer. She tried the Elizabeth Lake town office, but nobody answered there either. Then she got directory listings for Dr Candon and she recognised the voice of Alex's father as soon as he answered.

'This is Sarah Stellers. Is—is Alex there?'

'Hi, Sarah, how's the ankle?'

'I—fine.' She still hadn't sent him her medical number, she realised. 'Alex isn't there, is he?'

'No. He was earlier, but he's gone back to the office. Can I give him a message from you.'

'No.' She felt faint. He had been at his father's earlier, and now he must be on his way back to the office. He was not out flying anywhere, so they were searching for someone else. Not Alex. Not Alex's helicopter. 'I—I'll—no message. I'll call him later.'

Dr Candon cleared his throat. 'Well, he might be at the hockey rink tonight, so you probably won't get him until late. You're sure there's no message?'

'No. Thanks, and—and I'll send you my medical number. I keep forgetting.'

He said, 'No sweat, Sarah,' and she said a fairly calm goodbye.

She managed to put the receiver into its cradle before the tears came. That was crazy because she should have cried a long time ago. The phone rang and she ignored it and then the intercom buzzed and she pushed it and said, 'Nothing now, Brenda. Give me a while.'

It wasn't going to get better. Perhaps she would never be exactly the woman that Alex wanted, but she had to try because time would not change anything. Loving Alex would always be the most important thing in her life.

CHAPTER ELEVEN

IF omens meant anything, Sarah decided that the gods must be with her. The late-afternoon flight to Smithers was booked, but she went out to the airport and succeeded in getting a cancellation at the last minute. The jet flew her directly from Vancouver to Smithers airport, no snow and no detours. In Smithers the car rental representative met her with the promised car, complete with a map and a full tank of petrol.

Good omens. She needed good omens.

It was eight o'clock at night when she drove into Elizabeth Lake. This was not the same town she had visited back in January. This was a springtime place, the houses nestled in tall stands of evergreens. There was not a snowflake in sight in the town, although the hills between Smithers and Elizabeth Lake had been covered in white less than three months ago.

The road coming into town led past the hangar where she had landed in January. The runway was clear now, a bare, broad section of road that seemed to be disused for ordinary traffic. The two small planes which she had seen back in January were parked to one side of the hangar. She assumed that Alex's helicopter must be inside the doors of the converted barn.

No black truck. No BMW.

She drove on, through the main street. His truck was not outside the town office. Of course not. It was too late. He would be at home or else at that hockey practice. She doubled back towards the hill and passed Joyce walking along with a pram. Joyce turned and Sarah waved and told herself that it was too late to turn back now. She had been seen. Joyce would spread the word.

She drove up the same hill where Alex had found her the night he made love to her, when she broke her ankle running away. Running had been a mistake. She should have stayed and faced whatever the morning brought. Things might have been more straightforward between them in the last three months if she'd had the courage to face him the next morning.

She had been so afraid that he would reject her. She had given him her innocence and her unfolding love, and it was more than she had dreamed it could be. She had felt far too vulnerable to stand firm and wait for him to say goodbye.

She might be heading for exactly the same thing now. *Goodbye, Sarah.*

The garage door was smoothly closed. If there was a truck or car inside, she could not see it. She went up the stairs and rang his buzzer, but there was no answer. She tried the door, but his house was locked. Would she have had the nerve to open the door and go inside if it had been unlocked?

Perhaps.

She drove back down the hill. There wasn't that much to Elizabeth Lake, so Sarah began driving up one street and down the next, watching for the familiar truck. It didn't take long.

She found Alex's truck parked outside a big, low building that had to be the ice rink. There were other vehicles parked near by, two pick-up trucks and three cars. She parked between Alex's vehicle and a rusted orange station wagon.

There was no one at the entrance to the building, so she went in. At first she thought it was empty, unlocked but vacant. Then she found the bleachers and she saw people up in the stands. Ten or twelve couples, probably parents of the kids out in the rink.

There were two men out on the ice with the children. One of them was Alex. Sarah climbed up into the first row of bleachers, holding her breath as if Alex might hear her. The seats were all empty in this section. She sat down.

Alex was coaching a boy of eight or nine on how to handle his hockey stick. Sarah leaned back against the bleachers and watched, realising that it was perhaps the first time she had been free to observe him without his knowledge. He was very patient. Someone shouted something and his head lifted from the boy. The boy must have asked something, too, because Alex bent down to explain. Then she thought he smiled, but really it was too far away to be sure.

Someone blew a whistle and Alex patted the boy's shoulder, then skated away to the side of the ice. The boys on the ice sped around in a flurry that sent the hockey puck back and forth across the ice until someone fell and the whistle blew again. Alex and the other man spent some time with two of the young players, then they gathered the boys together in a group and Sarah could almost hear words, Alex's voice. Then the play started again.

This time the puck moved down the ice towards Sarah. The whistle blew when the boys had reached the goal just in front of where she was sitting. She watched Alex skate towards the boys. Towards her, but he had not seen her. He stopped with an effortless bit of magic with his skate-blades, then spoke for a moment to a couple of the boys. Sarah caught the words 'good play' and then he was moving again.

Skating straight towards her.

Sarah had thought that she was virtually invisible, tucked into the bottom seat near the edge of the bleachers. Alex skated down to the end and stopped with his hands on the wall between them, staring up at her. She tried to say hello, but her throat wouldn't move at all and she just stared down at him, trying to know what was in his face.

'Will you wait half an hour, Sarah?'

She nodded, unable to speak. She would wait forever.

She watched him working with the boys and the other two men who must be coaches, too, and, while she couldn't make her eyes move away from Alex, he didn't glance at her once. She waited and watched him and she hugged herself in the bleachers for warmth, but that was crazy because she had on her ski jacket and jeans and it was her heart that was afraid, making her shiver.

When the boys and the coaches skated off the ice the people down at the other end of the arena went out through what must be a door at the far end. Sarah was alone now, hugging herself and wondering if he had forgotten her.

She could get up and go and look, but he had asked her to wait and she could get lost in the catacombs that must be underneath the bleachers, where the skaters had disappeared.

When she heard a sound she turned.

Casey was running towards her. She was frightened for a second, but he was wagging his tail as he pushed his face up against hers. She put her arms around him, feeling his fur brush against her face. Then Alex was there and she stood, abruptly, her hand resting on the dog's head.

'Ready?' he asked. He did not come close enough to touch her.

She said, 'Yes,' and followed him.

The dog abandoned Sarah to run ahead of Alex. Alex was carrying his skates slung over his shoulder and the hockey stick in his hand. Outside he tossed the skates and the stick into the back of the truck and opened the passenger door for her to get in.

'I've got a rental car.' She gestured to the car and he followed her glance. She said awkwardly, 'I'll follow you.' She wished he would say something, wished he would touch her. She had thought he might be pleased to see her, but she could tell nothing from his face or his voice.

She followed his truck up the hill to his house. There was room in his garage for her car, so she drove in after him and parked between the truck and the BMW. He had brought the car back, she thought dully. Of course he had. He had changed his mind about needing to spend time in Vancouver. She had told him it was no use and he had driven away from her easily enough.

Too easily. If he let her back into his life now it would be her need more than his.

They went into the house together, Alex and Sarah and the dog between them. Casey went off into the kitchen, his footsteps echoing, and Alex said, 'If you give me time to clean up, I'll take you into town for a late supper. Have you had supper?'

'No. No, I haven't.' She doubted if she could eat.

He nodded and gestured towards the living-room. 'Make yourself at home,' he said, but she knew now that he didn't really mean it.

'When you say dinner in town,' she asked, 'what town do you mean?'

'Smithers. Elizabeth Lake's one dining place is closed by this time of night. Put on some music, Sarah. Drinks in the cupboard under the radio, if you want.'

When he disappeared into the back of the house she paced restlessly around his living-room. Music. She chose the album he had put on the evening he first took her in his arms. He might not recognise it, but it would be in her heart forever.

This was a terrible gamble. Eventually she would have to explain why she had come. What if she had to watch his face and his eyes showing impatience or pity, because he did not want the love she needed to give?

She took a big, ragged breath and took off her jacket. She looked at the drinks cupboard, but decided she needed her wits about her, so she went into the kitchen. Casey was there, wagging his tail and looking at her hopefully as if she might produce some doggy gourmet thing for him.

'Sorry,' she whispered, 'but nobody gave me free rein in this kitchen.'

She walked back to the living-room, then to the foyer. She picked up her jacket from the sofa where she had dropped it. She hung it up in the cupboard. She took her running-shoes off and put them in there, too, so that she was in stockinged feet again, vulnerable and afraid. She could not seem to stop prowling, but she did not have the nerve to go past the part of the house that she felt she had implicit permission to be in.

The living-room. The dining-room. The immaculate kitchen. Not back into the bedroom where he had carried her that night while she slept. She had seen his eyes tonight when he opened the door of the truck for her. She thought that she could be his lover again, but that had been a disaster, and would still be, because it simply was not enough.

She was at the kitchen window where she heard him. She spun around, her socks sliding on the waxed tiles of his kitchen floor. Casey stood up from the mat where he had been sprawled. Sarah spread her hands out behind her, feeling for the security of the counter, pressed against it, from the look in Alex's eyes, she must look terrified, as if she was about to run.

He was wearing corduroy trousers and a sports shirt with the collar open. She could see the dampness in his waving hair, and he must have shaved, too.

She said, 'I'm not dressed for any place fancy. For supper, I mean.' Her voice was husky, uncertain, and it was only words because he was dressed casually, too, but she wished now that she had not worn the jeans and the silky blouse that he had once said he liked so much.

'Come into the living-room, Sarah.'

She pressed back into the counter. The last time he had kept her in the living-room. Definitely only a guest, not someone who belonged. She whispered, 'Could I cook here?' She pushed her hair back uneasily. She had worn it down, for him, and she was afraid that that was a mistake, too. 'I—I'm not really a very experienced cook, but I'd like to...' Her voice faded to nothing.

'Why did you come? To see your aunt?'

She stared at his feet. He did not have shoes on either, just his socks below the cords, but it didn't make *him* look vulnerable.

She said, 'I heard this thing on the news. A helicopter. It was—missing. I thought—I was afraid——' She could not finish because what she had feared would be in her voice.

Alex said quietly, 'It wasn't me, Sarah.'

She whispered, 'If it had been...' And he didn't say anything and she couldn't look up at his face.

He asked tonelessly, 'What have you been doing?'

Missing you! She said huskily, 'Getting a new lift put in. Firing the chef. Just the normal stuff.' Was he going to stand there forever, not coming close?

'It doesn't sound much fun.'

'Pretty much as usual.'

'Sarah?'

'Yes.' She looked up and he was closer now.

'How long are you here for?'

She gulped. 'I—I can stay until Monday if—if I can make some phone calls. And—and I have to see Aunt Lori some time before I go.' She closed her eyes and offered raggedly, 'If you wanted me to come back, I could... I could come and...' Stay. She could not make herself say the word.

He took her face in his hands and she heard a cry torn from her throat and then she was in his arms, clinging to him, her arms around his neck and her face buried in his shoulder. He brought her close, or perhaps she pressed close, but then the tears started and she gulped, trying to stop them, but it was impossible, as if his arms had let loose all the pain she had held in.

He swept her up in his arms and carried her into the living-room, sat down in the big easy chair with her in his arms. 'Hush,' he murmured, stroking her hair back from her face and cradling her in his arms. She lay quietly, trying not to cry, but his lips moved over her face, kissing the tears away.

'Don't cry, Sarah. Tell me what it is and I'll make it right for you. Sarah——'

She tried to stop, felt a sob turn into a hiccup. 'I'm sorry. I know it's against the rules.'

He caught her hair then, pushing his hands through and tipping her face up for his inspection, saying raggedly, 'If we've got rules, you'd better tell me, hadn't you?'

She brushed her eyes with the back of her hand. She must look terrible, her eyes all red and swollen. She whispered, 'The rules of our affair. You don't want——'

'Rules?' Alex's voice was harsh, driven. 'When you walked into my life the rules all went out. I tried to keep my balance, but you've been able to drive me to madness from that first night.'

She whispered, 'You never told me!'

'Told you! My lord, woman! What do you think——? You've been fire in my blood from the beginning.' He closed his eyes tightly and said, 'If you hadn't come here I'd have been in Vancouver this weekend, trying to find a way into that closed life of yours. If I have to move into your damned hotel, I'll do that, but if there's any way you could let me work with you to create a place where we can be alone——' He buried his lips in her mouth and Sarah felt the thundering of his heart when she pushed her hands flat against his chest to give herself room to breathe.

She couldn't talk, could not think, because his eyes were neither cool nor closed now and she breathed, 'But you would never come into the hotel.'

He shifted her away and moved to his feet, pacing restlessly away from her. She would have felt terrified, alone, needing to reach for him, except that his eyes when he broke away from her were tormented and filled with something more.

'Your hotel.' He turned to stare at her blankly. 'It was the one place where I knew anyone could walk in or phone or say your name, and I'd lose. That's why I looked for you at that God-awful ball and not in your hotel.'

'You were jealous?' She said on a note of discovery. 'But Alex, how could you lose? Don't you know——'

'I lost in Charles's beach house. When the phone rang you didn't even look back when you went to take the call, didn't hesitate to go back, to leave me. When you said later that we should end it I knew you were right. I couldn't spend a life loving a woman who could walk away from me that easily.'

She whispered. 'Loving? Alex . . .'

He ground out, 'Loving. Yes. I came back here and did all the things that I'd told myself mattered to me, but I couldn't look at a telephone without fighting not to call you, and I couldn't sleep in my damned bed because you'd slept there! I got so desperate that I even—— Until you, Sarah, I never realised—I never knew I could feel the things you make me feel! I don't suppose there's anywhere in this world I can go where you won't haunt me.'

Sarah managed to get herself breathing. Her heart was hammering. She stood up and walked towards him, slowly, as if there were deep water she had to wade through to get across the carpet.

He was motionless, watching her with lowered brows. 'Ever since I met you I've been telling myself lies. I told myself I wanted you in bed, that I wanted an affair and you wouldn't really touch my life. It was a lie from the beginning. Nothing less than love would do—not with you.' His voice turned dark and violent. 'I never thought I was a jealous man, Sarah, but I'd burn that damn hotel down if I thought it would make you reach for *me* when you hear the telephone ring.'

She stopped a couple of feet away from him. 'Once, on the top of the mountain, I asked you if you planned to marry me.'

She saw him swallow and he said in a deep voice, 'I said no, Sarah, because I couldn't face a life as the man you walked away from when Stellers Gardens called. I knew about Kevin. He walked away when he lost, but I

was afraid I wouldn't be able to walk away at all and—
that terrified the hell out of me.'

She whispered, 'I didn't love him the way I love you,'
and the world went still. Even the music stopped.

He demanded, 'Say that again, Sarah,' and she heard
everything she would ever need in his voice. Her lips
parted, but his voice came out harsh. 'I don't know why
you asked me about marriage that night, but I thought
you might be going to tell me it was over if I wanted to
be more than your lover.'

She managed that last step and touched his chest.
'Alex, I've loved you from the beginning, but—I was
afraid.' He took her shoulders in his hands and drew
her close, staring down at her. She whispered, 'So could
we stay here for dinner? I really can cook, you know,
and ... well, I'd like to. I haven't had much chance to
be in kitchens.'

He laughed somewhere deep in his throat. 'If you tell
me you love me—you could give me burnt offerings and
I wouldn't care.' His eyes went flat and he asked, 'Would
you marry me?'

Sarah said, 'Yes,' but he seemed not to hear.

He brushed her cheek with his thumb. 'I have a friend
who's magic with management problems. I think he
could find a way for you to keep control of that place
and leave time—time for us to be a family.'

'Children?' she asked.

'Not if you don't want.' She knew from his eyes that
it was what he wanted for them. A family. Love and
warmth. She slipped her arms around his neck.

'Could we live here? I don't know much about being
a northerner, but I'd like to try.'

'Wherever you want.' He traced the curve of her lips.
'I'd better get something bigger than that helicopter,
though, to make it easier for us to get to Vancouver when

you need.' His thumb slipped between her lips. 'Not to mention a way to get you to civilisation when you get cabin fever.'

'I'm sure there would be fever, living with you.' Something flashed in his eyes and she flushed and whispered, 'I'd like children. Ours.'

He warned, 'Children take time, and so will I—maybe more than you'll want to give.'

She brought her lips up to his and saw love in his eyes. It had always been there, if she had found the courage to look. She said, 'I need your help on a valuation problem. I'm told you're an expert on stock evaluation. Will you do that for me?'

'I'd do anything for you, but—you're thinking of going public?' He was frowning. 'Your hotel's a family corporation, and solvent by all accounts. Why would you need to——?'

Sarah frowned. They had never discussed the hotel, but he seemed very knowledgeable about her financial affairs. She shook that question away and said, 'I'm not planning to juggle our marriage with the hotel, Alex.' She touched the place between his eyes and traced down the shape of his nose. 'I've received a buy-out offer. And—it's contingent on getting fifty-one per cent of the common shares. If I can talk enough of the family into voting for—I could be free of the albatross.'

'Albatross?' His hands slid down to her hips and she gasped at the intimacy of his body against hers. He growled, 'When did you start thinking of it as an albatross?'

'When my father died and left it in my hands.' She moved against him and knew that the words would end soon. 'Chains, and I couldn't seem to get free. Nobody was offering to buy in those days and what could I do but try to keep going?'

She threaded her fingers through the hair at the back of his neck and savoured the delicious thrill of knowing that soon he would not be able to wait any longer. His eyes told her that he would take her mouth, take her body in his arms, and make her truly his. Forever. She raised herself up on her toes and brushed heated lips against his.

He held her away from him as if that was the only way he could talk sensibly. His voice seemed oddly stilted. 'I don't want you making sacrifices, Sarah! You're not going to sell something that you'll regret later!'

'I'm only concerned with making sure I get a fair price. I don't want to feel guilty afterwards, because my family will do what I recommend, but it's their money too. You're rather an expert on stock valuation. You could help me see we don't get taken if you'd——'

'Albatross, you said?'

'Yes.' The time for talking was over now. She reached for the top button of her blouse.

Alex said harshly, 'You could have told me, not let me think I was trying to compete with a damned hotel. I—there's something I have to tell you.' She slid the first button open. He groaned, 'Sarah, if you...I hope you realise I'm not willing to put off our wedding. I want you *now.*'

'Yes,' she promised, opening the second button as she saw his eyes locked on her hands. She trembled at what she saw in his eyes. 'The only problem is that my mother is furious about Mike getting married in a register office in Halifax. She's sure to want to turn our wedding into a circus, but we can tell her to go hang.' She unfastened the last button and let the blouse fall to the floor.

'I don't give a damn if the whole of North America comes to our wedding.' His eyes had turned to flames.

'The more witnesses the better, just so it's clear that you belong to me. But there's something I have to tell you first.'

'I already belong to you,' she said huskily as her bra slipped to the floor.

She saw his hands clench in on themselves. 'Darling, if you—damn it! I—I'm the buyer.'

She froze. His eyes were dark and hard. 'That lawyer's letter? With the offer?' He nodded and she stammered, 'W—why?'

'I—I—oh, hell!' He shook his head and said in a harsh voice, 'A gamble, that's all. I got a look at the subscription list for your company, and you're not personally a majority holder. I had the crazy idea that the others might want to cash out, and then——'

'You hated the hotel. You said——'

'Did you think I went away and gave up, Sarah?' His face was harsh and his voice low and filled with pain. 'You'd have pulled me back, and I knew it. I couldn't stay up here and—if that damned hotel had to control your life, if I couldn't win against it——'

She smiled slowly. 'You were going to make yourself part of the hotel?' The controlling part, she thought with sudden, warm amusement. She told him softly, 'Help me find a manager.'

His breath went out in a long, harsh surge. 'Darling, I—you might change your mind, you might find you miss the excitement of hotel life once you've left it.'

She shook her head slowly, feeling excitement as his eyes followed the curves of her body. She said softly, 'I'll have no time for the hotel, not with you in my life.'

His eyes flashed, 'If you find later that you need...whatever you need—whatever you want, I'll give you.'

She whispered, 'You. I need you in my life...forever.' Her hands moved down to the fastener of her jeans.

He caught hold of her hands and brought them up to his cheeks. 'Sarah, stop! I want to unwrap the rest of my present myself.'

The telephone rang as she went into his arms. She reached her lips up and pulled him down to her with eager arms. 'Don't answer it,' she murmured. 'Please don't answer it.'

He drew her with him across the room to the telephone. She stared down at it, wishing it would stop. Alex kept one arm around her waist as he reached down and quietly unplugged the phone from the wall. Sarah felt her heart begin to beat again.

'Now, darling,' he said softly, 'I'm going to show you exactly how much I've missed you.' Then he swept the woman he loved up into his arms and carried her to their bedroom.

Next Month's Romances

Each month you can choose from a world of variety in romance with Mills & Boon. Below are the new titles to look out for next month, why not ask either Mills & Boon Reader Service or your Newsagent to reserve you a copy of the titles you want to buy — just tick the titles you would like to order and either post to Reader Service or take it to any Newsagent and ask them to order your books.

Please save me the following titles:	Please tick	√
THE WIDOW'S MITE	Emma Goldrick	
A MATTER OF TRUST	Penny Jordan	
A HAPPY MEETING	Betty Neels	
DESTINED TO MEET	Jessica Steele	
THE SEDUCTION STAKES	Lindsay Armstrong	
THE GREEN HEART	Jessica Marchant	
GUILTY PASSION	Jacqueline Baird	
HIDDEN IN THE PAST	Rosemary Gibson	
RUTHLESS LOVER	Sarah Holland	
AN IMPOSSIBLE KIND OF MAN	Kay Gregory	
THE WITCH'S WEDDING	Rosalie Ash	
LOVER'S CHARADE	Rachel Elliot	
SEED OF THE FIRE LILY	Angela Devine	
ROAD TO PARADISE	Shirley Kemp	
FLIGHT OF SWALLOWS	Liza Goodman	
FATHER'S DAY	Debbie Macomber	

If you would like to order these books from Mills & Boon Reader Service please send £1.70 per title to: Mills & Boon Reader Service, P.O. Box 236, Croydon, Surrey, CR9 3RU and quote your Subscriber No:..(If applicable) and complete the name and address details below. Alternatively, these books are available from many local Newsagents including W.H.Smith, J.Menzies, Martins and other paperback stockists from 9th October 1992.

Name:..

Address:..

....Post Code:.........................

To Retailer: If you would like to stock M&B books please contact your regular book/magazine wholesaler for details.

You may be mailed with offers from other reputable companies as a result of this application.
If you would rather not take advantage of these opportunities please tick box ☐

WIN A TRIP TO ITALY

Three lucky readers and their partners will spend a romantic weekend in Italy next May. You'll stay in a popular hotel in the centre of Rome, perfectly situated to visit the famous sites by day and enjoy the food and wine of Italy by night. During the weekend we are holding our first International Reader Party, an exciting celebratory event where you can mingle with Mills & Boon fans from all over Europe and meet some of our top authors.

HOW TO ENTER

We'd like to know just how wonderfully romantic your partner is, and how much Mills & Boon means to you.

Firstly, answer the questions below and then fill in our tie-breaker sentence:

1. **Which is Rome's famous ancient ruin?**

   ❑ The Parthenon   ❑ The Colosseum   ❑ The Sphinx

2. **Who is the famous Italian opera singer?**

   ❑ Nana Mouskouri   ❑ Julio Iglesias   ❑ Luciano Pavarotti

3. **Which wine comes from Italy?**

   ❑ Frascati   ❑ Liebfraumilch   ❑ Bordeaux

Tie-Breaker: Well just how romantic is your man? Does he buy you chocolates, send you flowers, take you to romantic candlelit restaurants? Send us a recent snapshot of the two of you (passport size is fine), together with a caption which tells us in no more than 15 words what makes your romantic man so special you'd like to visit Rome with him as the weekend guests of Mills & Boon.

....

....

....

....

Mills & Boon

In order to find out more about how much Mills & Boon means to you, we'd like you to answer the following questions:

1. How long have you been reading Mills & Boon books?

☐ One year or less ☐ 2-5 years ☐ 6-10 years

☐ 10 years or more

2. Which series do you usually read?

☐ Mills & Boon Romances ☐ Medical Romances ☐ Best Seller

☐ Temptation ☐ Duet ☐ Masquerade

3. How often do you read them? ☐ 1 a month or less

☐ 2-4 a month ☐ 5-10 a month ☐ More than 10 a month

Please complete the details below and send your entry to: Mills & Boon Reader Service, FREEPOST, P.O. Box 236, Croydon, Surrey CR9 9EL, England.

Name: ....

Address: ....

.... Post Code: ....

Are you a Reader Service subscriber?

☐ No ☐ Yes my Subscriber No. is: ....

_____ RULES & CONDITIONS OF ENTRY _____

1. Only one entry per household.
2. Applicants must be 18 years old or over.
3. Employees of Mills & Boon Ltd., its retailers, wholesalers, agencies or families thereof are not eligible to enter.
4. The competition prize is as stated. No cash alternative will be given.
5. Proof of posting will not be accepted as proof of receipt.
6. The closing date for entries is 31st December 1992.
7. The three entrants with correct answers who offer tie-breaker sentences considered to be the most appropriate and original will be

judged the winners.
8. Winners will be notified by post by 31st January 1993.
9. The weekend trip to Rome and the Reader Party will take place in May 1993.
10. It is a requirement of the competition that the winners attend the Reader Party and agree to feature in any publicity exercises.
11. If you would like your snapshot returned, please enclose a SAE and we'll return it after the closing date.
12. To obtain a list of the winning entries, send a SAE to the competition address after 28th February, 1993.

You may be mailed with offers from other reputable companies as a result of this application. Please tick the box if you would prefer not to receive such offers. ☐